T0328503

Praise for
The Journey's End

Babila Mutia's *The Journey's End* is a classic! His creative and imaginative genius is at play as he adroitly demonstrates that joy and pain can shake hands at some point but never an embrace. Lucas Wango and *Général* epitomize these two polarized worlds in the novel.

—**Kehbuma Langmia**, author of *Takumbeng* and *Evil Feeds on Itself* (Langaa)

***

Mutia's writing continues to examine the human condition through his carefully crafted characters which are presented to the reader in astonishing social, cultural and emotional detail. *The Journey's End* takes on some challenging themes not least those of a society encountering urbanisation at pace and all that it has to offer as well as all that it might take away.

—**E. Dawson Varughese**, author of *Beyond the Postcolonial* (Palgrave Macmillan)

***

The Journey's End is an enthralling and all-embracing story, brilliantly written and skilfully blended with an enriching cultural repertoire. Ba'bila Mutia masterly represents the complexities of the contemporary social, economic and political realities of a country that is smeared with degradation and drudgery.

—**Charles Ngiewih Teke**, Literary Critic, University of Yaounde I

***

Ba'bila Mutia handles words as a gifted sculptor would handle clay. This story is bittersweet, tender, often wickedly humorous and almost certain to elicit tears. After reading this novel, you will never look at everyone who comes into your life in quite the same way.

—**Victor N. Gomia**, Department of English and Foreign Languages, Delaware State University

THE
JOURNEY'S
END

The Journey's End

Ba'bila Mutia

SPEARS
MEDIA PRESS

SPEARS MEDIA PRESS

7830 W. Alameda Ave, Suite 103 Denver, CO 80226

Anembom Consulting Building, Cow Street, Bamenda

P O Box 1151, Bamenda, NWR, Cameroon

Spears Media Press publishes under the auspices of the Spears Media Association.

The Press furthers the Association's mission by advancing knowledge in education, learning, entertainment and research.

First Published 2016 by Spears Media Press
www.spearsmedia.com
info@spearsmedia.com

Information on this title: www.spearsmedia.com/thejourneysend
© Ba'bila Mutia 2016
All rights reserved.

Ordering Information:
Special discounts are available on bulk purchases by corporations, associations, and others. For details, contact the publisher at any of the addresses above.

ISBN: 978-1-942876-09-0 [Paperback]
ISBN: 978-1-942876-10-6 [Ebook]

For
Maboh, Luma, Liga,
Mammy Rufina, and
Andin (who did not live to read this story)

Acknowledgement

I would like to extend my gratitude to the Rockefeller Foundation for the one-month residency at the Villa Serbelloni in Bellagio that enabled me to finish writing this novel.

ONE

The pensioner first met the disabled man at the Anguissa junction. It was a chance meeting that would change the lives of both men. The pensioner came out of the taxi at the wrong place. Too late, he realized he was at the Nkolndongo junction. Since arriving Yaoundé, he had always confused the IPTEC College junction at Nkolndongo with the Anguissa junction.

He adjusted the raffia bag hanging from his shoulder and looked around him, trying to get his bearings. He was a bald, stocky old man with a receding forehead and big ears. What was left of hair on his head formed an atoll-shaped tuft at the back of his head. There were deep furrowed lines at the edge of his sunken jaws; and perfectly symmetrical lines on both sides of his forehead ran parallel to his grey, bushy eyebrows. His dark aged face was bedecked with a big nose and flared nostrils that had the shape of twin megaphones.

He looked to his left and saw the Oilibya Filling Station in the distance. That was the direction towards Mvog-Mbi. Anguissa was to his right then. He waited for a gap in the line of passing cars before he crossed the street. Suddenly, it started raining. He had not expected the rains to start so early, in mid-May, so he did not bring an umbrella. He adjusted the bag on his shoulder and bent down to retie the lace of his right shoe. He was wearing an old threadbare suit and black shoes he had bought at the used shoe market. The shoes were covered in the copper-brown mud of the afternoon's rain. After he fastened the lace of his right shoe, he folded up the leg openings of his trousers to just below his knees, exposing a pair of brown cotton socks. He straightened up and readjusted the bag; then he re-tucked in his faded blue shirt beneath his belt. He adjusted his tie and began walking towards Anguissa. He was oblivious to the muddy rainwater from gaping potholes that passing cars splashed on him as he looked out for the familiar landmarks that would indicate he was on the right street.

Torrents of rainwater had excavated the sides of the thinly paved street, leaving rough jagged islands on both sides of the road. The pensioner now walked more slowly, looking left and right on both sides of the street. He saw *Garage Beti, Pharmacie La Balance, Florida Bar, Le Debrouillard Bar,* as he walked along. He observed the rows of old wretched houses that bordered the street. Occasionally, he wiped off the raindrops on his face with his right hand. A smile of relief spread across his face when he saw the bold familiar *Siata Peinture* and *Boulangerie du Stade Malien* signboards. On his left, he saw *Froid et Comfort,* the refrigerator repair shop with its carcasses of abandoned refrigerators. The initial shower was now giving way to a drizzle. He noticed the *Boulangerie Moderne* to his left as he steadily made progress towards Anguissa. He went past a shoe repair store and a makeshift roadside restaurant in a wooden shack. By the time he got to Anguissa, he was tired, and his legs were hurting.

He crossed the street and walked straight into the *Rio bar d'Anguissa.* A large wooden canopy covered with aluminium roofing had been constructed as an extension under which the bar's clientele sat outside, drank beer and observed life on the street. The pensioner went directly to the wooden counter.

"*Oui, Monsieur?*" the boy behind the counter said in French.

"Let me have a Beaufort," the pensioner said. He spoke in a high-pitched, muffled tone, partly because he had lost some of his teeth.

The boy opened a freezer, brought out a Beaufort, opened it, and glided it across the counter. "Five hundred francs, *Monsieur*."

The pensioner reached into his bag and brought out a crumbled one thousand francs note. He gave it to the boy. The boy pulled a drawer behind the counter, brought out a five hundred francs coin and handed him the change. He took the beer and went outside to the veranda, under the canopy. He sat down on a long wooden bench facing the street. Then he remembered that he should have asked for a glass. He shrugged his shoulders, lifted the bottle, and tilted its neck to his lips. His Adam's apple rose and fell as he savoured the refreshing flavour of the beer gurgling down his throat. He lowered the bottle, looked at it briefly, and put it down on a wooden stool in front of him. He felt relieved for the moment as he looked around him.

For the first time, he noticed that the bar was at the junction. Almost directly opposite him, a vendor was selling imported apples and cigarettes. His gaze moved away from the junction and dwelled briefly at the signboard that read *Garage du Renouveau*. There were abandoned trucks and cars in the fenced enclosure that made up the mechanic workshop. Four young boys, dressed in brown, grease-stained overalls were hunched over the engine compartment of a white Peugeot car. He also noticed a tyre repair service beside the garage. Stacks of imported second-hand tyres were conspicuously displayed in front of the roadside shack that housed the repairman and his equipment. Behind the garage, away from the chaos of the Anguissa intersection, the pensioner's gaze fell on a four storey marble house that was in its last stages of completion.

He looked at his watch. It was getting close to 5:30 PM. He took his time to finish the remaining beer before he brought out a handkerchief from his left trouser pocket and wiped his mouth. He stood up and walked out of the bar. It had stopped raining. He was just about to step into the street when he heard the voice of a man appealing for help. The pensioner turned his head to the right and looked down. That was when he saw the disabled man.

He sat on the muddy stretch by the road. The brown shorts he wore exposed the shrivelled ligaments of his twisted legs and thighs. Two black rubber pads were stuck on his bony knees. The pensioner was about to pass when the disabled man's voice halted him in his tracks.

"You, sir, help a poor beggar. Five hundred francs, anything you can spare. Or a thousand francs and I will tell you your fortune and future."

There was something authoritative, a forceful imperative in the beggar's voice which the pensioner could not resist. He turned round again and looked at him. The disabled man raised a plastic bowl and held it up with his right hand. He had thick forearms, a broad chest, and beefy biceps. He would easily have passed for a boxer if his legs were normal. His face had a calm and ancient mien with a deeply mystical patience written all over his placid countenance.

The pensioner reached for the change in his bag. He brought out a 100 francs coin and dropped it into the beggar's bowl.

"A hundred francs!" the disabled man cried. "Not enough! This can't buy me a loaf of bread or even a beer."

The pensioner dipped his hand again into his bag and brought out a five hundred francs coin. He dropped it into the beggar's bowl. The disabled man scooped out the coins and stuffed them away, somewhere in the voluminous brown shirt he wore. He looked up at the pensioner and a toothy smile spread across his face.

"Thank you, brother," he said, "thank you for your generosity."

"We must thank God for everything," the pensioner replied.

"You're a man of God then?" the disabled man interjected.

"We're all children of God," the pensioner responded, "destined to help each other."

"Then God has sent you to me. Destiny has knocked on your

door this evening." The pensioner looked puzzled. "Come with me," the disabled man commanded.

The pensioner hesitated. "It's getting late. I must get to where I'm staying." He walked towards the street and was about to cross to the other side.

"I say, come with me." There was that commanding tone in the disabled man's voice again. "You're from the Public Service, aren't you? From the Ministry. Following up your pension file. I say come with me."

The pensioner stopped and turned round slowly as if hypnotized. Several cars began hooting furiously. A taxi driver pushed his head through the window and shouted an obscenity at the old man. It was then he realized he was in the middle of the street. He jumped back to the muddy sidewalk and stood in front of the disabled man again.

"Who are you? How did you know who I am and what I'm doing here?"

"Your fortune and your future," the disabled man said. "He who gives generously receives generously. Now, follow me. You have nothing to fear."

The disabled man brought out two U-shaped fabricated wooden contraptions from beneath the folds of his shirt and turned them upside down. He gripped them with both hands and transferred his body weight from his buttocks to his knees and the wooden props. Then he began creeping on all fours along the muddy sidewalk. It was then the pensioner saw the thick black rubber pad that was fitted underneath his scrawny buttocks. With the aid of his wooden supports and rapid propulsion of his padded knees, the disabled man moved rapidly along the street.

The disabled man turned his head over his shoulder and glanced at the old man. "Hurry up, and stop staring at me like that. If it were not of this rain and mud, I could move faster than this." He wriggled along, his body writhing like a worm. He dashed to the middle of the street, raised his right hand, and waved the wooden prop in the air.

"The cars!" the old man shouted, fearing he was about to witness a ghastly accident. But the disabled man ignored him. The traffic on both sides of the street stopped abruptly as if someone had given them an invisible signal. The old man scurried after the disabled man. He barely caught up with him at the other side of the street. As soon as the disabled man had safely crossed the street, the traffic resumed as usual. None of the motorists said a word. Some pedestrians who had watched the crossing quickly turned their heads away when the disabled man raised his head and looked at their faces.

"And where are you taking me to?" the pensioner asked. There was a note of anxiety in his voice. "It's getting late."

"To my headquarters, my work place. Don't be afraid. Everyone in Anguissa knows me."

The pensioner followed the disabled man hesitantly. They passed a mud and wooden house beside the road. The owner had placed five mounds of sugar cane and four big stones to prevent road-users from encroaching on his land. They skirted the house and came to a kolanut tree. There was an old kerosene drum under the tree. The two men moved on. Soon they came to a single grave decorated with white ceramic tiles. Months of dust and rain had ruined the whitewash that had been used to paint the top of the grave. The disabled man advanced rapidly along a small beaten track that ran opposite the grave. They passed another wretched and uninhabited mud and cardboard house. Finally, they came upon a small clearing behind the cardboard house. The pensioner was surprised to see a yellow shipping container at the edge of the clearing.

"There," the disabled man announced triumphantly. "That's my headquarters." The old man had barely been able to keep up with the disabled man's pace. He was panting heavily and was completely out of breath as he followed the disabled man. Approaching the container, the pensioner saw a white, rectangular sign-board stuck up against a small tree beside the container.

GRAND GUERISSEUR
(Herbalist, Occultist, Seer, Spiritualist)

* * *

Specialist in Protection
Medicine Against Witchcraft
Poison and Accident
Venereal Diseases
AIDS
Gastritis, Hypertension, Eye Diseases
Sterility and Impotence

"What's this?" the pensioner asked. "Where are we?"

The disabled man did not answer. He raised himself up to the container and released a latch. A door that had been cut from the side of the container swung open. The disabled man raised himself up and placed his buttocks on the lower ledge of the door. Then he used his right hand and dragged his feet after him. The pensioner cautiously walked up to the open door. He took a look at his watch. It was almost 6 PM. Because of the surrounding trees and vegetation, it was already getting dark.

"You can come in," he heard the disabled man's voice from inside. "There's no one else inside here."

The pensioner walked through the door and stepped into the interior of the container. It was dark inside, and he could no longer see the disabled man. A momentary flutter of fear seized him. He turned round quickly and was about to run away when he heard the disabled man's voice again.

"It's dark inside here. I'll turn on the light."

A single fluorescent bulb flickered momentarily before its white light came on permanently. The pensioner blinked as his eyes adjusted to the sudden brilliance of the light. When he stopped blinking, he saw the disabled man seated in a wheelchair at the far corner of the container. The sticks he had been using and the rubber pads that were stuck on his buttocks and knees lay on the floor. A large bookcase with several books occupied a wall, behind the disabled man. A calendar, a business licence and a large framed photograph of the head of state hung on the wall beside the bookcase. On his left was a small table littered with files, papers, ink bottles, rubber stamps, a cellphone, and other assorted office equipment. There were two wooden boxes behind the table. Several stools and three upholstered chairs were neatly arranged along the walls of the container. The pensioner also noticed a window on the wall opposite the door. The window was shut.

The disabled man watched the amazement and surprise on the face of the old man with detached amusement. A faint, bemused smile hovered around the corners of his mouth as he regarded the pensioner. He skilfully manoeuvred the wheelchair and moved it to the table. He opened a drawer, brought out a pair of gold-rimmed reading glasses and put them on.

"What kind of place is this? What ... what do you do?" the pensioner faltered.

"Won't you sit down first?"

"Yes, yes." The pensioner sat down on one of the chairs.

"I transact all my business here." There was a thrill in his voice.

"That sign out there—" the pensioner began.

"Yes," the disabled man said. "I'm a spiritualist, a seer, and a healer. But I do several other things as well."

"You mean you ... you're not a beggar?"

The disabled man laughed aloud, revealing two perfect rows of white teeth. He took off his glasses and put them on the table.

"I used to be a beggar. A long time ago. But that's another story."

"How did you know about me? What I came to do here?"

"You mean your pension file in the Public Service?" The disabled man laughed again. "It's my business to know what people come to do in Yaoundé. I've got several sources, some human, others spiritual."

He adjusted the wheelchair and rolled it towards one of the boxes. He leaned forward slightly towards the smaller box. He fumbled around in the box for a few moments and brought out a human skull, the remains of a desiccated chameleon and several cowries. He closed the box and transferred the strange paraphernalia to his left hand. He pushed the right wheel of his chair with the other hand and came out from behind the table. He placed the skull and chameleon on the floor in front of the pensioner. Next, he transferred the cowries from his left to his right hand. He looked intently at the pensioner's face for almost half a minute and then closed his eyes.

His eyes stayed closed for about three minutes. Then his eyelids began to quiver. When he opened his eyes, his face had undergone a remarkable transformation. There was a trance-like expression on his countenance. It was as if an arcane blanket had suddenly been pulled over his conscious mind. Slowly, he shook the cowries in his cupped right hand a number of times before he threw them on the bare floor. He studied the pattern of the shells on the floor intensely and then he looked at the pensioner again.

"You're from Yambe, in the North West region."

"Yes, yes," the pensioner responded eagerly.

The disabled man gathered up the shells, shook them three times and threw them on the floor again. He studied the pattern and looked at the old man.

"You retired from the civil service a long time ago."

"Yes," the old man responded.

The disabled man gathered up the cowries and shook them

twice before he threw them again on the floor. He looked at them intently and glanced at the old man's face. "Seven years!" he exclaimed. "You've been following your pension file for seven years! It's still in the Public Service."

The old man leaned back in his chair and took in a deep breath. "I don't know what to do," he said. "I may die without getting a single franc from my pension money."

The disabled man did not seem to hear what the old man said. He looked at the cowries on the floor for the last time and gazed at the old man. "Everyone at home in your household is fine and well."

The old man craned his neck and looked at the strange pattern of the cowrie shells on the floor in wonder.

The disabled man kept his head still for a while as he closed his eyes again. A few minutes later, he shook his head slowly and wiped his face with both hands. He appeared to have come out of a trance. He picked up the cowries, the desiccated chameleon and the skull, turned the wheelchair round and returned the objects to the box.

"How long have you been doing this? I mean, seeing into the unknown and the past."

"And the future too," the disabled man said as he glanced at his watch. "It's getting late. Do you really wish to stay and hear my story?"

"Yes," the pensioner said. "It's not quite often that one meets people like you."

The disabled man rolled the wheelchair nearer the table and put on his reading glasses again. He fidgeted around for a while. He seemed to be searching for something.

"I can't find my national identity card," he said. "But does it matter? It's the only clue to my heritage, where I came from, who I was. It's more than ten years old. I haven't bothered to change it."

"And what has your identity card got to do with what you do

here?" the pensioner wanted to know.

The disabled man removed the glasses from his face and put them down. He adjusted the wheelchair, fixed his left elbow on the table and held his chin with his index finger and thumb.

"It reminds me of how I came here. It's the only reminder of who I was that's still left. Like you, I came to Yaoundé many years ago. Ten years? Twelve? Fifteen? I can't remember. My father died soon after I graduated as a teacher from TTC, the Teacher Training College in Moghamo. I was a young man then. I was sent to teach in a government secondary school near my hometown. As his successor, I was to be initiated into the secret society of palace notables to which my father belonged. Our tradition required elaborate death and funeral celebrations to usher him into the ancestral world. For more than six months I had no salary. I wrote several letters to the Ministry of Secondary Education, to the Public Service, and to the Prime Minister's Office. I wrote more letters, petitions and pleas, to find out what was happening to my file. I received no response to any of those letters. Another six months passed. I needed my accumulated salary very badly. I had to celebrate my father's transition into the land of our ancestors. I had to go to Yaoundé. Going to Yaoundé became a do-or-die trip. My entire life and my family name depended on my going to Yaoundé. Never in my life had so much depended on one journey. But why ... why am I telling you all this?"

There was a vague expression of nostalgia on the disabled man's face. He seemed to be looking at the pensioner, but he was actually staring beyond the old man, into the past he thought was buried forever. Over the years, he had tried to run away from these memories. He dreaded moments like this when he had to face himself, when he was compelled to grasp intangible wisps of smoke that had dispersed into the emptiness of a dead past.

TWO

The Moghamo Government Teachers' Training College was built on a low plateau that overlooked the terraced patches of farmland stretching along the entire Moghamo plain. It was a blend of stone buildings, plastered mud-brick houses, and modern concrete architecture. The students' dormitories were near the staff quarters, next to the eucalyptus plantation from which the college got its firewood. The average age of the students was about 24-years. Most of them were already quite mature by the time they came to Moghamo.

They had just finished writing their final teacher training exams and were waiting for the results and postings to the various schools where they would be sent to start their teaching careers. Akuma was at Unity dormitory with his friends when Sambeng came looking for him. It was almost 7 PM. His friends were playing a game of cards, waiting to go to the common room to watch the 7:30 PM CRTV news in English. Akuma was reading a book as usual.

"Akuma," Sambeng called him as he entered the dormitory, "the principal wants to see you at once."

Akuma lowered the book he was reading and looked at Sambeng. The other students stopped the card game they were playing.

Akuma stood up. He was of average height with square, sturdy shoulders and a round face. He closed the book and put it on his bed. "Where's the principal?" he asked Sambeng. "Where did you meet him?"

"He's waiting for you in his house. I met him in front of the administrative block," Sambeng said.

"What else did he say?" Akuma wanted to know.

"It looks as if he was coming here when he saw me," Sambeng said. "He wants you to meet him at home."

"Did he say anything, why he wanted to see me?" Akuma asked.

"No," Sambeng said.

Akuma looked at his watch. It was getting close to news time. "Let me go and find out what fate awaits me in the principal's house," he told the other boys. "I wonder what I've done this time. I hope I haven't failed my final exams."

"Come on, Akuma," one of his friends said. "You know you're the best in the class. The day you fail an exam the world will come to end."

Sambeng pulled a chair and sat down with the other students as Akuma went out. Akuma took a short cut behind the library that took him past the refectory, through the basketball court to the staff quarters. When he knocked on the door to the principal's house, it was the principal, Ebenezer Jatto himself, who opened the door.

"Come on in," he urged Akuma. "Don't bother to remove your shoes. Come right in." Akuma tried to read the principal's face for any clue about the sudden summon as he stepped in his sitting room. That was when he saw his uncle, his father's only brother. He was standing by the cupboard close to one of the windows. The sight of his shabby uncle in the luxuriously carpeted surroundings of his principal's house embarrassed him. For a moment, he stood transfixed at the doorway. There was an apologetic expression on his face as he looked at the tattered shirt, the patched trousers and dusty rubber shoes his middle aged uncle wore. The hat on his head was full of moth holes, and he clutched his old raffia bag close to his body with nervous fingers. He was still blinking at the unfamiliar glare of the fluorescent lights in Mr. Jatto's house.

"What's the matter with you?" Mr. Jatto said. "Won't you greet your uncle?"

Akuma forced a smile as he walked up to his uncle. "Uncle Kewa," he managed to say in his local language, "what ... what brings you here? Is everybody at home okay?"

"We're all fine and well," his uncle said. "How are you?" He stretched his hand and greeted him. There was no warmth in his uncle's handshake. His voice was hoarse and shaky. He could not look Akuma straight in the face.

"I think you should sit down for a moment," Mr. Jatto said. "Your uncle came in about fifteen minutes ago. I'm afraid he's got bad news for you."

Bad news? The only bad news that would bring someone as elderly as his uncle to look for him in school would be a sudden death in the family. He first thought of his mother, his father's third and last wife, who was forty-two. She was rarely sick and seemed immune to the common ailments that plagued the family, including malaria. Was it an accident? He forced the thought out of his mind. His father's other two wives, perhaps. They were much older, the first in her late fifties, the other getting close to fifty. And then, of course, there was his maternal grandmother who was in her eighties. Even if she had died, they would not send someone as important as his uncle.

"What has happened, Uncle Kewa?" he asked. Even as he asked the question, a chill ran through his body. He had experienced that chill ever since he was a child. Anytime he felt like that, he sensed the shadow of death close by. He tried to push the thought from his mind. "Is someone very sick? Has there been an accident?"

His uncle returned his inquiring gaze with an impassive face. Akuma thought he detected a trace of inevitability, of loss. The old man clutched his bag with his left hand in an effort to restrain his emotions. Akuma rushed up to him and held him by the forearms.

"What is it, Uncle Kewa? Tell me the truth! It's Pa, isn't it? He's dead. It's him, isn't it?"

"It's not that bad," the principal said. "Your uncle has been on the road since two in the afternoon. Your father is very sick. He was taken to the mission hospital in Acha Tugi. There's been no improvement, so they've taken him back to the village."

"My father has never been sick before," Akuma told Mr. Jatto. He turned his head and tried to study the features on his uncle's face, to see whether he could detect the slightest trace of concealment on the old man's rugged expression. "You must tell me the truth, Uncle Kewa. If my father has died, I have the right to be told at once."

"I can't tell you a lie, my son. Your father was admitted into Acha Tugi for close to a month. We spent so much money, but his condition didn't improve. It only grew worse, so we took him back to the village to see a traditional doctor. Three days ago he could not talk or recognize the faces around his bed. It was only yesterday that he opened his eyes and looked around. The first word he uttered was your name. He wants to see you. You must come home at once—"

"What kind of illness is it? What have the doctors said?"

"I'm afraid this is no time for questions, Akuma," the principal said. "If your old man was not seriously sick, your uncle wouldn't be here."

"You're no longer a child, Akuma," his uncle said. "Your father is close to 65 years old now. He's not as strong as he used to be and certainly not as resistant to illness as he's been all these years. You must prepare yourself for the worst. It will be a miracle if we find him alive when we get home."

The chilly tremor ran through Akuma's entire body again. He felt his head spin as he listened to his uncle's voice. There was an unexplained heaviness, a kind of weight he had never felt before on top of his head. He tried to visualise his father's face. He suddenly had this feeling of floating, a disembodied emptiness. He tried to force himself to say something, but his mouth was dry. He looked around for a chair and sat down wearily.

The principal looked very concerned. "Are you okay?"

Akuma heard the principal's voice from a distance. "Yes, yes," he forced himself to talk. "I'm ... I'm fine sir."

His uncle turned to the principal. "We're wasting valuable time. We have to leave at once."

"All the way to Menamo? You know what time it is?" The principal looked at his watch. "It's close to 9 PM. You can't risk travelling in the night. There's nothing both of you can do to help the situation. But I certainly won't allow a student of this college, even with a critically ill father, to take the risk of night travel."

"Akuma is my brother's first and only educated child," Kewa explained to the principal. Then he hesitated. There was no way the principal would understand the urgency of a dying man requesting the presence of his only educated son around his death bed.

"You'll have to spend the night here at the campus, I'm afraid," the principal cut in. "Both of you will leave tomorrow as early as 4 AM."

Kewa turned and looked at his nephew who slumped in the chair. He turned round again and faced the principal. He felt trapped and helpless by the rigid regulations of an educational system that could not comprehend his culture and traditions.

"No! I say no!" Kewa shouted. "You have no right to deprive a son of receiving the last blessings from his dying father. We'll leave at once! Right now!"

The principal was taken aback by the sudden change in Kewa's demeanour. "All right, all right," he said cautiously. "It was only an advice. I didn't intend to interfere. Of course, you're free to leave with the boy. After all, they're through with their final exams."

"Thank you, sir," Akuma managed to say. He had recovered some of his composure.

"I'm sorry about the bad news," Mr. Jatto said. "But you've got to put on a brave face, you understand."

"Yes, sir. Thank you, sir."

Akuma and his uncle left the principal's house and went to the dormitory for Akuma to park a few clothes. Akuma's friends were sad to see him leave, but he told them he'd be back in a week or two. His father was sick. He had to go and see him.

Kewa didn't say a single word to Akuma during the entire journey. Akuma didn't know why he kept on thinking of the stories his grandmother used to tell him when he was about six years old. She used to tell him stories about when he was born, where their people came from, why his father's compound was next to the Fon's palace. She told him stories about various rituals he used to witness when he was a boy. Tuginam, as their Fondom was called, was an assortment of thirty-five villages that were made up of the Saba and Jemki clans. The two clans occupied large stretches of land in the North and in the South that ran along the fertile plain of the Ngora River. Their present traditional leader, Fon Akwafe II, lived in Menamo, his home village, the biggest village in Tuginam.

According to his grandmother, Nwi, the Divine creator, who created the first humans and animals, endowed the Ngora plain with animals of various shapes and sizes—buffalos, deers, porcupines, dogs, pigs, horses, lions, panthers, monkeys, squirrels, and many birds. In those days, humans did not die but lived forever. People became so old and tired of life that they complained a lot, wishing their very long lives would come to an end. Finally, they called on Nwi to take a decision on their lives.

Nwi asked them to send Him two animals to His celestial kingdom. When the animals would get to his spiritual abode, He would take a final decision on the matter. The people of Tuginam selected the dog and the chameleon and dispatched them to see Nwi. When the dog and chameleon reached Nwi's kingdom, Nwi gave them two messages. The dog was to tell the people that they would continue to live forever while the chameleon was to tell the people that they would die in their old age. Nwi would confirm the decision of the one that reached first. The chameleon and dog left Nwi's kingdom and headed back to Tuginam. Since the dog was quite agile, he moved faster and soon left the chameleon behind; but the chameleon took his time. When the dog got to the outskirts of Tuginam, he was attracted by a big bone with large chunks of meat which someone had thrown by the wayside. The dog stopped and began eating the bone. While the dog was busy eating, the chameleon passed him and headed to the Fon's palace where he delivered the message Nwi had given him to the Fon. As soon as the chameleon delivered the message, Nwi decreed that humans will no longer live forever but will die in their old age.

Akuma recalled his grandmother telling him that it was for this reason that the Tuginam people hate chameleons. Wherever they see a chameleon, they must kill it.

* * *

They arrived Menamo at 3 AM. The full moon had kept vigil with them throughout the entire journey. The night sky was illuminated by thousands of stars he only seemed to notice now. The starlight silhouetted his uncle walking beside him. His uncle lagged a few steps behind, the first indication that the long trek had finally taken its toll on the aging man. He recognised the vast stretch of farmlands that indicated the outskirts of the village. He heard the first cockcrow in the distance.

"We're not too far from the main market square and the Fon's palace," he said, breaking the long silence between him and his uncle. He partly talked to himself, letting his uncle know that the topography of the land was forever imprinted in his mind. His uncle did not reply. He appeared to be lost in his own thoughts. Soon they reached the main market square. The Fon's palace was to the left, slightly elevated on a small plateau. They passed by several more compounds and silhouettes of plantain, banana, coffee, and cassava farms before they reached his father's compound. His attentive ears picked up an isolated cough and the rustle of animal or human footsteps somewhere nearby. Another cockcrow. And then he saw his father's house loom in front of him. It was the main house in the compound, set apart from the other smaller houses of his father's three wives.

His uncle entered the house first, and he followed behind. He took in the details of the room as he came in. They had moved his father's bed into the main living room. There were several relatives keeping vigil. They sat on the floor in a variety of reposes around the bed. Most of them were asleep. Others were barely awake. His mother and two stepmothers were among the relatives. His father's two sisters were also there. A small kerosene lantern that hung on the wall illuminated the room, casting exaggerated, grotesque shadows on the walls. The subdued light from its lowered wick accentuated the gloomy atmosphere in the room. Tenuous wisps of smoke rose lazily from a dying fire at the far left corner of the living room. The fire had kept the house warm for some time during the night. Now the remnants of whatever embers were left in its ashes left no warmth in the house. It was his mother who first saw him. She stood up and embraced him. Akuma felt love, concern, and then despair, all in one moment, in his mother's affectionate embrace. He glanced at her momentarily as he approached his father's bed. He sat down on the bed.

His father's face had become emaciated. His body frame was smaller. The angular and stern features of the face were still there, but they were no longer imposing as they used to be when Akuma was a child. His eyes were closed and his breathing was steady.

Kewa walked up to the bed and addressed the old man. "*Mo.* It's me, Kewa. We have arrived. Your son from Moghamo is here." The figure in the bed did not stir. Kewa addressed his brother again, raising his voice slightly. "It's me, Kewa, your brother. I say Akuma is here, sitting near you, on the bed."

"Father," Akuma said. His voice was hoarse and shaky. "Father, it's me. Akuma. Can you hear me? You sent Uncle Kewa to fetch me from the college."

The old man stirred and his eyes fluttered. He opened his eyes and his head moved slightly. He stretched his right hand slowly and touched his son. He opened his mouth as if to say something. Then he was seized by a fit of coughing.

"It's the cough," he heard his mother say. "It's become worse over the months."

"Father," Akuma said, "how do you feel?"

He stopped coughing and his Adam's apple moved up and down twice before he spoke. "My son. You've come." His voice was frail. It sounded hollow as if it came from a distant location that was unconnected with his body. "At last, you've arrived. Thanks to *Nwi* you've ... you've met me alive." He was seized by another violent fit of coughing. When he stopped coughing he said, "It's my chest. Something is choking me inside. They took me to the hospital in Acha Tugi—" He began to cough again.

"You should try and go back to sleep and allow your son to rest," a female voice suggested. "They've been trekking all night. You can talk to him later in the day."

"No. No, I can't ... I can't wait." He struggled to raise a feeble hand so that he could sit up. Akuma put his left hand round his shoulders and propped him up to lean against the twisted pillow on which his head was reclined. "Where are you, Kewa?"

"I'm here, *Mo*," Kewa answered from where he sat.

"Is Yensi there?"

"I'm here," Akuma's mother answered.

"What about Yenika and Dora?" the old man asked, referring to his two sisters.

"They're both here, *Mo*," Kewa said.

"Who else is in the room?"

"Yaje and Majah, your other wives and some relatives," Kewa said. "Is there anything in particular you want, something you want us to do?"

"Let the relatives go out. I want a few minutes with my son. There're important family matters I want to … to discuss with him. Kewa, you can stay. Yensi, Yaje, and Majah too can stay. And my two sisters."

The rest of the relatives who had woken up during the conversation filed out slowly from the house. As soon as the last one went out, Kewa closed the door.

"They've all gone, *Mo*," Kewa said.

"Akuma."

"Father."

"The hour of the great journey is finally at hand. I never knew it would come so early. But I've done my best in life. The things I couldn't finish doing, you'll finish them. I thank *Nwi* for having a son like you who has acquired a good education. What did you study in Moghamo?"

"I was trained to become a teacher," Akuma answered. "We finished writing the final exams a month ago. I expect to pass. Then I'll become a teacher."

"A teacher? Kewa."

"*Mo*."

"Did you hear that? A teacher. The first teacher in … in our family." He began to cough again. When the coughing subsided, he said, "You're the only hope we have now in the family. Do you hear me?"

"Yes, father."

"What was I saying? Every time I close my eyes, I meet those who have passed before. I've met Nah Manyi, my grandmother, who died when I was only ten. I've also seen my father too and many others who have gone before me. My departure is at hand."

"Don't say such things," Yensi interjected. "You're just having bad dreams. It means nothing. You'll get better."

In spite of the visible pain on his countenance, the old man forced a smile. "Look at my wasted body? Is this the body of a man who'll get better? There're things to be said and done. Kewa," he called his brother. "Where are you?"

"I'm here, *Mo.*"

"Listen very carefully. I'm entrusting this boy in your hands. You have to guide him. Do you hear?"

"As you say, *Mo.*"

"The first thing is the succession to replace me in the *Kwifor*, the secret society that enthrones the Fon and guards the ancient secrets of our people. You must ensure that he ...he is my successor. I've already sent word to the palace and ... and to the other eleven *Kwifor* notables." He began to cough again.

"Try and rest," Kewa said. "The talking is not good for you."

"Just one ... one or two more details. Then I'll go back to sleep. Is Yensi there?"

"I'm here," Akuma's mother answered.

"Go and fetch Sirra's parents. Let them come along with the girl." Yensi got up, went out of the house, and closed the door gently behind her.

The old man stretched his frail hand and held his son. "Akuma."

"Father."

"You've always been a peacemaker in the family. You've never discriminated between your real mother and ... and my other two wives. You've always called all ... all of them 'mother.' You enter and eat in each ... each house without discrimination. Most importantly, you'll soon become a ... a teacher. You're now the head of the family. You know I'm ... I'm leaving behind several cows and farmlands. Four houses. You must ensure that there's no ... no in-fighting among your brothers and sisters. You hear me?"

"I hear you, father."

Yensi came back to the house as they spoke, followed by Pa Watechi, his wife, and Sirra, their eldest daughter. Akuma's face lit up as soon as Sirra entered the house. They had grown up and played together as children, but she was about five or six years younger than him. During the last long holidays, he had visited her a number of times in her compound. And he had written her two letters when he went back to Moghamo. She was now a mature woman. The waning light from the kerosene lantern prevented him from fully appreciating her features. The only visible details were her broad shoulders, full bust, and shapely wide hips. She wore a wrapper and looked sleepy. They must have woken her up barely a few minutes ago. The three of them sat down on the bamboo stools at one end of the room.

The old man noticed the look on his son's face and a faint grin appeared on his face. "I see you ... you both know each other," he said weakly, glancing at Sirra, and addressing his son. "Pa Watechi, I'm sorry to ... to get you up at this early hour of ... of the morning."

"We were awake," Pa Watechi said. "We've been waiting the whole night. It's only Sirra we had to get up.

"How are you, Sirra?" the old man inquired.

"I'm fine, *Mo*," Sirra answered. Her voice sounded gentle and soothing, a little bit unsure about what to say in this unusual circumstance.

"I wanted both of you here together," the old man began, addressing Akuma. "It's good Pa Watechi and ... and Sirra's mother are here. Pa Watechi told me about the ... the letters you wrote to Sirra when you left the village and ... and went to Moghamo. While you were away, before this sickness began, I ... I took the initiative to knock Pa Watechi's door and engage Sirra for you. A marriage between the two of you will ... will only strengthen the long friendship between our families. And I want to assure Pa Watechi that Sirra is ... Sirra is getting married into ... into a reputable ... to ... to an educated young ... a young man with ...

with a bright...."

His voice faltered as he spoke and his head slumped on his chest. Akuma was alarmed. He held his father's hand and tried to lift up his head. Kewa rushed forward and propped his sagging shoulders.

"*Mo*," Kewa said, "You're too tired to continue talking. Lie down and rest for a while. We've all heard what you've said."

The old man gathered his ebbing strength and struggled to raise his head. He raised his right hand and beckoned Sirra to come to the edge of the bed. Sirra walked up to the bed and sat near Akuma. Akuma felt the heat from her body engulf him as she sat down next to him. An imperceptible, enigmatic smile hovered around the corners of her wide mouth as she took a furtive glance at Akuma's face. The old man took her hand and placed it on top of his son's hand. Akuma felt the uncomfortable bulge of a stiff erection as Sirra's large soft palm engulfed and squeezed his hand, sending a warm seductive radiation through his body. He glanced momentarily at the full curve of her breasts before he turned his attention to his father's face.

The old man withdrew his hand, lowered his head back on the pillow, and closed his eyes.

"Father!" Akuma called. "Father!" There was a note of panic in his voice.

"I'm tired," the old man's voice echoed back. "I'll sleep now."

Kewa motioned to Sirra and her parents that they could now depart. Sirra rose slowly from the bed. She took one last look at Akuma before they went out.

"Father!" Akuma called again. "Father!" The old man did not answer. Akuma felt his pulse. It was feeble but throbbing steadily.

"He's sleeping," Kewa said. "You can go now to your mother's house and get some sleep before dawn." Kewa raised his right hand as Akuma tried to protest. "I'm also exhausted from our long journey in the night, but I'll stay here with the rest of the family.

Tell the other relatives to come in."

Akuma stood up reluctantly and walked out of the house. He dropped off into an uneasy sleep as soon as he got to his mother's house. He had barely fallen asleep when he found himself in the dream world, walking with someone he thought was his uncle. The dream seemed to be a replay of the long night trek with his uncle from Moghamo until he realised that the man walking with him was his father. They walked in silence, not talking to each other. The trek seemed endless as they walked across several hills and valleys. Then the scenery changed to a vast countryside of cornfields interspersed with wild flowers. An endless swarm of bees buzzed with a persistent drone that became a monotonous hum. The strange unattended cornfield stretched to the horizon, in each direction, as far as the eye could see. The cornfield gradually merged into a large field with pink and red lilies. The field was demarcated by a small shallow brook with clear crystal water that flowed lazily through the lilies. The sun was to the East, but it appeared to be setting instead of rising because its light was of a muted golden hue, casting no shadows, and penetrating both the lilies and the brook, making them sparkle. There was a long wooden fence at the other side, running parallel to the brook; and there was a stile on both sides of the fence. It was when Akuma and his father waded across the brook that he heard the enchanting voices and musical instruments of what sounded like a welcoming party and a celebration beyond the fence. When they came to the fence his father stopped and spoke for the first time.

"We'll part company now. The journey ends here for you." He held his son's hand. "You've been a most worthy companion and I thank you for the company." Akuma tried to protest, saying that he would continue the journey, but his father refused. "You'll go back. I'll climb the fence and move on alone. They're waiting for me on the other side. You've got a lot to do in the morning, so go back now!"

With that last word his father began climbing the wooden stile. When he got to the top of the fence, he turned round and looked at his son one more time. There was an intimate, nostalgic look on his face. Akuma watched him descend the other side and walk away towards the singing voices and the music.

Then he woke up. He heard the subdued wail of female voices coming from the direction of his father's house. He got up quickly and went outside. The wailing voices were distinctly audible. Yes, they were in the direction of his father's house. He ran across the small courtyard that separated his father's bigger house from the rest of the smaller houses of his mother and stepmothers. He met Kewa at the front entrance, coming out of the house.

There was a grim look on Kewa's face. "He's gone," he said with a note of finality in his voice. "He departed just about an hour ago. I'm going up to the palace to inform the Fon. Go in and wait for me. I'll be back soon."

Kewa moved away as Akuma walked into the death house and saw his father from a distance, lying inert, face upwards. He moved closer and sat down on the bed. He found it hard to believe that this was the same man, who, hours ago had been talking to him. He suddenly felt dizzy as he stared at his father's immobile face. His arms and knees grew weak. Since men were not supposed to show any emotion in public, he struggled to hold back the tears that were welling up in his eyes. Because of the polygamous nature of his family, he had always felt close to his mother than his father; but seeing his father lying lifeless on the bed, stirred up some deep emotions inside him. He could not fight the tears anymore.

Akuma was in a trance-like state during the activities that marked the first stage of his father's transition. The events passed on slowly, like a film before his eyes. At times, he felt he was an actor, an unwilling participant in a bad movie; but most often he found himself a mere spectator, uninvolved in both the direction and production of the film.

Kewa came back half an hour later with Pa Sumbu, the most elderly member of the *Kwifor* secret society. Pa Sumbu held a black metal gong and was accompanied by two of the Fon's retainers to see the corpse and confirm that Akuma's father had really died. Each of the retainers held a bundle of seven spears neatly tied together to look like one spear. The spearheads were wrapped in white sheep skin and adorned with a long red tassel. Since by tradition the Fon was prohibited from seeing a corpse, the two bundles of spears and the retainers were an expression of the Fon's presence. Kewa and the three men entered the compound in silence. The wailing in the death house stopped as soon as Pa Sumbu and the retainers walked into the compound. When they entered the death house, Pa Sumbu walked round the corpse two times, each time going into the opposite direction and muttering some incantation which was not audible to the family members in the room. After this brief ritual, he signalled the two retainers who had been standing by in silence that they could now go. As soon as they went outside, Pa Sumbu began beating the metal gong with a hard wooden baton that was devised for that purpose. It was a steady beat that produced a hollow metallic sound. He would continue the beat as he moved round every village footpath and road with the two retainers. Anyone who heard the sound of the gong or saw Pa Sumbu and the retainers with the bundle of spears knew at once that they announced the passing away of either a notable or a member of the *Kwifor* secret society. Within a few minutes, the sound of the gong had faded in the distance.

"What do we do now?" Akuma asked Kewa, as soon Pa Sumbu and the retainers had departed. "What happens to the body?"

"By tradition, the Fon is not allowed to see any corpse. The two retainers will go back to the palace and inform him that your father has passed away. We shall await the arrival of members of the *Kwifor* secret society. They're the only ones allowed to handle your father's corpse. Our family will be given until 2 PM to mourn him. Thereafter, the funeral arrangements will be left in the hands of the *Kwifor*. We won't be allowed to touch his corpse again."

"What about Pa Sumbu?"

"He'll part company with the retainers at the entrance of the Fon's palace. While the retainers go to confirm the death to the Fon, Pa Sumbu will go to the *Kwifor* secret shrine on the outskirts of the village and beat the secret drum. By midday, the rest of the eleven members of the *Kwifor* who represent the original founders of the twelve clans of our people will assemble at the shrine to start preparing for the funeral rites. They would come here by 2 PM. But I'm sure the *Kibarankoh* will make its appearance before they arrive. From experience, it will be a dreadful spectacle."

By 7:30 AM, the compound was full of relatives who had heard about the death. Most of the women sat on the floor, inside the death house, wailing. The men sat outside on bamboo stools talking in subdued voices. The rest of the relatives and sympathizers sat in the other houses of the late man's wives, the women inside, the men outside.

Akuma grew up calling his father *Mo*, like the rest of the family members. Later on, at about the age of eleven, he came to learn that *Mo* was not a name but a title for notables and family heads. Thereafter he began calling him 'Father' without actually knowing his real name. It was his grandmother, his father's mother who eventually told him that his father's real name was Fontamo Njebufah. His father had inherited this strange name from the legendary warlord who had led their ethnic group into battle along the Ndop plains and defeated the combined armies of the Tonyi, Mbenka, and Wiiring tribes. Fontamo Njebufah literally meant "the spear that is thrown and never touches the earth." But no one ever called him Fontamo Njebufah. Later on, when his second wife bore him a set of twin girls, everyone started calling him *Tangyi*, meaning father of twins.

"Your father has many names," Akuma's grandmother said one evening. "Only the other eleven members of the *Kwifor* secret society know his real name. No one else does. Even the Fon doesn't know his name. We shall only know his real name on the day he departs to meet the ancestors." Akuma was old enough to know that "meet the ancestors" meant the day his father will die.

Time seemed to drag on with an agonising slowness. More people came to their compound as news of his father's death spread in the village. Around 11:30 AM, the *Kibarankoh* emerged from its secret shrine. Two elderly men with clean-shaven heads heralded the arrival of the masquerade. They ran about 50 metres ahead of the *Kibarankoh*. One held a spear and the other a metal gong that he beat continuously with a small wooden baton to alert people on the road that the dreaded masquerade was approaching. They ran back and forth, their bloodshot eyes peering at the curious onlookers and passers-by as they shouted out repeated warnings that the masquerade was not too far away.

The *Kibarankoh* ran forward leaving a whirlwind of dust behind as it jumped from one side of the road to another in a display of power and agility. Its mask was old and hideous. The expression on the mask was a grotesque combination of torment, antiquity, and deformity. The raffia fibres on its body were old and covered in soot. The legs of the man who was inside the masquerade were black and flaky, like a reptile. The masquerade left in its wake a strong nauseating stench that forced people to cover their noses. Two women vomited in the bushes as the *Kibarankoh* passed. Bits and pieces of the masquerade's flaky body fell on the road as it made its ferocious progress to the dead man's compound. Its ferocity was restrained by three very long ropes attached to its waist and held by three hefty youthful men who strained to keep the masquerade under control. Occasionally the *Kibarankoh* turned round in a fit of anger and chased its three attendants who fled in fear and abandoned the restraining ropes. The *Kibarankoh* took advantage of this brief moment of freedom to terrorise the population. It uprooted a mature plantain stem from the earth and flung it several metres in the air. The attendants quickly ran back and took control of the ropes again as they strained hard to restrain the *Kibarankoh* from destroying the village. This scenario went on for half an hour as the masquerade and its attendants made their way through the village, past the government secondary school, the main market and the Fon's palace. When they got to the ceremonial grounds in front of the palace, the *Kibarankoh* spun round, apparently confused about which way to go. Then it dashed in the direction of the palace. The attendants pulled on the ropes and shouted out an order. The masquerade turned round and headed in the opposite direction. By this time, a large crowd of mostly children and men had joined the spectacle. The crowd tagged along from a safe distance as the masquerade made its way to Njebufah's compound.

When the *Kibarankoh* got to the dead man's compound it circled the house three times, attempting to demolish it with its bare hands. Each time the hefty young men strained at the ropes as they struggled to hold the masquerade from wrecking havoc in Njebufah's compound. On three occasions, the *Kibarankoh* let out a dreadful howl as it cried out to the attendants to let it go, to allow it run amok and grapple with the beast called death. Each howl was a frightful moan that chilled the blood of the onlookers. In one last effort of defiance, the masquerade turned round and pulled two of the ropes that restrained it. The two attendants at the end of the ropes fell on the ground. The third man fled in panic. Then all hell broke loose. The *Kibarankoh* seemed to momentarily gyrate on one spot, spinning on its own axis like a demented dervish. Round and round it spun, picking up speed and momentum. Then in one final frenetic motion of demonic energy, it leaped in the air, completely defying the law of gravity, and landed on the roof of one of the houses in the compound.

The terrified mourners screamed in bewilderment as the *Kibaran-koh* systematically tore down the grass roof of the house with its bare hands. It leaped in the air again from the roof and landed on the ground, the grotesque face of its ghastly mask searching for a new target to assault. It charged in the direction of a small crowd of intrepid onlookers who had been foolish enough to hang around. The curious onlookers scattered in all directions, stumbling over each other in panic as the *Kibarankoh* bore down on them. It chased them down the road that led away from Njebufah's compound. The three attendants emerged from where they had been hiding and gave chase. After a while, they secured the ropes again and managed to take control of the masquerade. One by one, the terrified mourners began coming back to the compound. The departure of the *Kibarankoh* was as dramatic as its arrival. Within a few minutes, the sound of the metal gong announcing its departure receded out of earshot.

The 11 members of the *Kwifor* arrived just before 2 PM. Their arrival was less spectacular than that of the *Kibarankoh*, but it was solemn and ritualistic. Passers-by along their path gave way and stooped silently in awe and reverence as the *Kwifor* made its progress across the village. They were all elderly men, way past their seventies. Pa Sumbu led the group as they slowly made their way to Njebufah's compound. They each held a sturdy wooden staff that they pounded on the ground as they marched in rhythmic steps into the dead man's compound. They were shirtless. Each of them wore a red and black cloth which was folded under their legs and tugged behind their waists. They each had a leaf stuck in their mouth and each man wore an ivory bangle on his right wrist.

The women in the main house of the dead man did not wait for the *Kwifor* to reach the compound before filing out in small groups. The increasing regular thud of the *Kwifor* staffs as the men approached was enough. They all knew the culture. By the time the *Kwifor* got to the compound, Njebufah's house was already empty. His corpse lay alone on the bed in the middle of the house as the *Kwifor* entered the house. Akuma observed that they all left their wooden staffs outside, at the right side of the door as they entered the house. The crowd of mourners outside and in the surrounding houses waited patiently for the men to begin performing the secret rite that would usher Njebufah to the next world. The silence was intense and deep. The waiting crowd outside heard the muffled resonance of Pa Sumbu's voice as he pronounced the secret incantations in the death house.

Soon after, the eleven men began filing out. Pa Sumbu held a small calabash of water when they emerged from the house. Akuma noticed that the leaves that were in their mouths when they came to the compound were no longer there. Led by Pa Sumbu, the eleven men walked round Njebufah's house first clockwise, seven times, and counter-clockwise seven more times. Each time, Pa Sumbu dipped his right hand into the calabash and sprinkled water around the house. Then they assembled at the front door, one by one before they went into the house again. A few minutes later four of the notables came out and positioned themselves by one of the windows of the house. The other men inside lifted Njebufah's corpse and sent it out through the window to the other members of *Kwifor* who were waiting outside. The corpse was wrapped in a raffia mat. Two other notables came out to assist the four men outside to carry the dead man. The rest of the men came out of the house, one after the other. Pa Sumbu was the last to come out. He handed each man his staff as they got ready to depart with the corpse. When they were ready to go, Pa Sumbu stopped momentarily and looked at the mourners for the first time.

"Chemufor finally makes his exit from this compound this afternoon," Pa Sumbu said,

A great cry rose up from the crowd. The women ululated and banged whatever instrument or implement was at hand—pots, metal plates, hoes. The men hollered. The cry reverberated through the crowded compound in waves—first from the women then to the men and back again to the women, this time, accompanied by children. A stray dog in the crowd began barking furiously.

Kewa turned to Akuma. "This is the moment we've all been waiting for. As soon as you succeed your father, when your position as the twelfth member of the *Kwifor* is confirmed, you too will be given a secret name, known only to you and the other eleven notables. That has been the tradition."

"Those who departed before us wait for him in another compound," Pa Sumbu continued. "This is a journey, not a disappearance."

A great cry rose again from the crowd.

"A beginning, not an end," Pa Sumbu carried on with the incantation. "An arrival, not a departure. Chemufor goes where he began; he will begin again where he's going."

Once again the thunderous shout from the mourners reverberated in the compound.

"*Kwifor* does not die," Pa Sumbu carried on, "we only regenerate ourselves. From this world into the next, from the next world into this one. So Chemufor is not dead. He leaves this compound to the next to rest for a while before he returns. He will wake up again and be recognised in this same compound by those of us who know him."

The last shout from the mourners was more subdued. The *Kwifor* departed with Njebufah's corpse from his compound. They went back again to the village, to their grove where they would perform secret pre-burial rites before burying the dead man. It was barely ten minutes after their departure that a big downpour descended on the village. The heavy rain was accompanied by ominous peals of thunder and blinding flashes of lightning.

A vague, uneasy emotion of inevitability, of an inability to affect circumstances beyond his control gripped Akuma. Every single face and sensation that afternoon was transformed into a haunting memory—the agony of loss; the anguish on his mother's face; Kewa's trembling body; the stupor of hopelessness on the faces of his step-brothers and sisters; the twisted figures of his aging stepmothers sprawled on the ground; the sunshine and the beautiful rolling hills in the distance; the contrasting blue sky before the *Kwifor* came; the unexpected heavy rains that soaked the mourners to the skin; the gushing rivulets of brown muddy rain water in which he used to navigate paper boats when he was a child. The impressions piled upon themselves, one after the other until his forehead was about to explode. The events of that afternoon, that day, in particular, would remain etched in his mind forever.

Later in the night, there was a full moon in the sky when he went to look for Sirra in her father's compound. He had told her he would come to see her around midnight. She was waiting for him when he arrived. The night was cool and quiet. She led him to the grass underneath the mango tree behind their compound. She untied the coloured loincloth she was wearing and spread it on the grass. They sat for a long time, not talking, only holding hands. Later on, she undressed slowly, letting him soak in the beauty of her body, in a momentary attempt to distract his wandering mind from the loss he was trying to cope with. When she was completely naked, Akuma buried his face in her breasts and cried for a while. She held his head and caressed his hair gently. The love-making, later on, was gentle at first. But the pace quickened as Akuma became aroused and excited by Sirra's passionate moans that urged him to quicken his pace. Her broad hips underneath him wriggled upwards meeting each of his pelvic thrusts in a counter motion. Her big hands gripped his body as she urged him on with endearing words and whispers of secrets only she alone knew. The sheer ecstasy and the sensuous exhilaration were overwhelming as Sirra's gyrating rhythm threatened to engulf him. He could resist her no more. Moments later, his whole being disintegrated into one enormous explosion of multiple states of consciousness. Then a sublime bliss he had never known in his entire life settled over him.

Akuma soon dozed off. When he woke up, Sirra was gone. He found himself alone, lying naked on the coloured loincloth underneath the mango tree. He suddenly felt exposed and vulnerable. He stood up and put on his clothes quickly. He was quite relieved that no one had noticed his absence when he got back to his father's compound.

* * *

Akuma went back to Moghamo three weeks after everyone in his immediate family, including himself, had shaved their hair to the skin as part of the mourning ceremonies for his late father. His mother and two stepmothers, his siblings, his half-brothers and sisters, his maternal and paternal aunts and uncles—everyone was obliged to shave their hair. He did not know his father had so many relatives until that day. The day before he left for Moghamo, he came to his late father's main house where his widowed mother and stepmothers sat on plantains leaves on the floor. The widowhood tradition prohibited widows from shaking hands during the period of six months when they would mourn their husband. They were also forbidden to sit on chairs and eat from plates during this period.

Akuma greeted his two stepmothers as he pulled a small bamboo stool and sat next to his mother. She had taken care of his father throughout the three months he was admitted to the hospital in Acha Tugi, always by his side, never thinking that she was going to lose him. His death and the events of the past few weeks had taken their toll on her. Her face was strained with exhaustion, making her look much older than she really was.

"I intend to travel to Moghamo tomorrow," he told his mother.

She looked up at his round face. She was surprised that he was going back so soon. "I thought you had finished writing your final exams," she wondered aloud.

"Yes," he said. "I have to go back to Moghamo to know whether I passed or failed the exams."

She lifted her right hand and held his left forearm momentarily. She wanted to tell him that she felt somehow deprived of his affection. They hadn't had enough time together to talk about family matters and other things a mother always talked with her son. She remembered how they used to chat in the evenings when she came back from the farm and cooked the evening meal, long before he was admitted to the government teacher's training college. It seemed like decades ago. How time had deprived her of her son. And now her husband was gone. She was about to say something but changed her mind. She closed her half-open mouth and turned her eyes away from him.

"Go on Mother. You wanted to say something."

"No," she said. "Nothing of importance. I know you'll pass your exams. That's what I wanted to say."

"The results should be out by now. I'm sure the postings, the lists of the various schools we would be sent to teach, have already been released by the Ministry. The earlier I get back to Moghamo, the better. My box containing my clothes and books is still there. I have to bring it home."

She nodded. "I'm sure I'll not see you before you leave," she complained.

"No. I'll leave very early, by the first cockcrow."

"And you'll not have time to eat something—"

"It will be too early to eat, mother. I'll buy some food along the road before midday."

"Don't stay in Moghamo for long."

"I won't, mother. I know a lot of things await me here. Uncle Kewa has told me that there're several things to be done."

"You'll visit the Fon in the palace when you come back, won't you?"

"I know, mother." There was a trace of impatience in his voice. "I won't be in Moghamo for more than a week."

"One whole week! Have you seen Sirra and her mother?"

He stood up. "Not yet. I'll see them right away, in a few minutes." With that last word, he walked outside. It was already dark. He switched on the flashlight he was holding and watched its beam slice a bright ray of light through the woolly darkness outside. He selected one of the several paths and that led to Sirra's family compound.

* * *

Akuma was invited to the Fon's palace three months after his father's burial, long after he had returned from Moghamo. The eleven members of the *Kwifor* were already seated on carved stools when he was ushered into the Fon's audience hall. The twelfth stool on which his father used to sit was vacant. Pa Sumbu, the eldest member of the *Kwifor* pointed to an ordinary chair on which Akuma sat down. They all waited for about half an hour before the Fon came out from his inner chamber. When he entered the audience hall, Akuma and the eleven members of *Kwifor*, clapped their hands three times, as a sign of respect for the Fon.

"I hope you slept well, *Mbeh*," Pa Sumbu said.

"Yes, indeed. I slept quite well," the Fon said. He sat down on the royal throne before he asked the rest of the men to sit down.

The Fon turned to Akuma. "Your father's death came as a surprise to the palace. I didn't imagine his health was that serious when he was taken to Acha Tugi hospital. He wasn't that old, I believe."

"He was only sixty-five *Mbeh*," Akuma said.

"He was a well-respected and dynamic man in the palace,

particularly when it came to matters of dealing with the government administration and arbitration of land conflicts with our neighbours. We shall all miss him in the Fondom."

"Thank you, *Mbeh*."

"While he was alive he informed the palace that you'll be his successor in the family and his replacement in *Kwifor*. Are you aware of that?"

"That's what I've been told, *Mbeh*."

"As his successor, you have the sole responsibility to organise his *cry-die* when the time comes. The community shall join you in the celebrations, but you're the one that everyone will look up to. Pa Sumbu, you have something to say about this, don't you?" The Fon turned his head and looked in the direction of Pa Sumbu.

Pa Sumbu cleared his throat, clapped three times, before he said, "Yes, *Mbeh*, I have. The *cry-die* and the departure rituals that will usher Chemufor to the world of our ancestors are supposed to take place six months from the day he was buried. His successor has to provide six goats, ten chickens, four drums of palm oil, six jugs of palm wine, and twenty crates of beer as his family's contribution to the funeral ceremony. I'm sure he knows that half of each of these items will be sent to the palace. It is only after Chemufor's departure rituals are performed that Akuma will be secretly initiated into *Kwifor* and recognised as his father's rightful successor."

"You've heard what Pa Sumbu has said," the Fon said.

"Yes, *Mbeh*, I've heard," Akuma said.

The Fon stood up. Akuma and the eleven members of *Kwifor* rose to their feet and clapped their hands three times, bowing their heads slightly as the Fon walked out of the audience hall.

Akuma left the palace and decided to go directly to Pa Watechi's compound. He took a short cut from the palace that took him straight to the compound. It was already midday.

When he reached Sirra's father's compound he went directly to the main house in the middle of the compound. Pa Watechi was having his afternoon meal when Akuma walked into the house. He was happy to see Akuma. "My son-in-law," he said with delight, "sit down and share this afternoon meal with me. I'm so glad to see you." He raised his voice and called Beri, Sirra's younger sister.

When Beri entered the house she said, "Yes, Papa."

"Where's Sirra?"

"She went out, Papa."

"Where to?"

"I don't know, Papa."

"Tell your mother to send more corn *fufu* and *njama-njama*. Tell her we have a guest."

"Yes, Papa," she said and went out.

A few minutes later she came back with two bowls, one with the corn *fufu*, and the other with the vegetable. She placed both bowls on the table and walked out politely.

"Pull your chair nearer and help yourself with the *fufu* and *njama-njama*."

"Thank you, Pa." He pulled his chair towards the small stool, dished a good portion of the vegetable and began eating it with the corn *fufu*. "It tastes delicious, Pa. Who cooked it?"

"Can you guess who?" Pa Watechi asked.

"Your wife, Sirra's mother."

Pa Watechi grinned. "You're wrong," he said. "It's Sirra. You won't believe it. She cooks like her mother."

"Don't say!" Akuma exclaimed.

"It's a wise choice you've made, getting married to my daughter."

"I think so, Pa. I'm a lucky man to have found a wife like Sirra."

When the food was finished, Pa Watechi called Beri to take away the dishes. As she walked out of the house, Pa Watechi asked Akuma whether he would drink some palm wine.

"How old is the palm wine, Pa?" Akuma asked.

"Almost a day old. I tapped it myself from my palm trees. It's been in the house since yesterday morning. But it's fresh and cool."

"Since yesterday? I won' try it, Pa. I don't want to leave your compound drunk. People will wonder what kind of son-in-law Pa Watechi has accepted into his family."

Pa Watechi laughed boisterously. "You'll make a good husband for my daughter," he said, "a very good one. By the way," he said, switching the topic of conversation, "where have you been sent to teach? I hear your teaching posts have come out."

"I was posted to Government High School, Meghani."

"The people of Meghani are our neighbours."

"Yes," Akuma said. "Meghani is about fifteen kilometres from our village. In the dry season, it takes only thirty minutes to get there by bus. Now in the rainy season, with the mud and steep hills, it takes any time from four to eight hours to get to Meghani."

"I see." He kept quiet for a few minutes before he said, "You know it was your late father who approached me and said he wanted you to marry Sirra. He actually initiated the process and carried out the *knock-door* in your absence. But he didn't finish paying all the things for the *knock-door* and bride price."

"I didn't know that, Pa. I thought he had finished everything concerning the *knock-door* and bride price. How much was left?"

"A hundred and fifty thousand francs plus four tins of palm oil. Two tins to my brothers and the other two to my half-sisters. The actual traditional marriage can only take place when you finish paying the money and provide four tins of palm oil."

"Listen, Pa Watechi. I know it's important for me to finish paying the bride price and to provide the four tins of palm oil before I marry your daughter. I really want to marry Sirra before my father's *cry-die*. You're a father to me now so I must tell you the truth."

"What are you talking about?"

"We expected our first salaries three months after our

graduation. We all sent our integration files to Yaoundé. The Ministry promised us that we would have our salaries within three months."

"What has happened?"

"It's now getting to five months and I've not yet heard from Yaoundé."

"That's a serious matter."

"It is, Pa. Very serious."

"What do you intend to do? You can't function without a salary."

"I can't, Pa. That's why I'm going to Yaoundé."

"To Yaoundé? When?"

"Next week. The earlier, the better. There're too many things I have to do. I need money to do all of them. Without my salary and the arrears, I'll accomplish nothing."

"I didn't know this was the situation."

"It is Pa. There're only two people in whom I've confided my trip to Yaoundé. My half-brother, Fabian the carpenter, and yourself. Not even my mother knows that I'll go to Yaoundé. I'll simply disappear from the compound. I've told Fabian to tell my mother that I've travelled to Yaoundé if she becomes alarmed by my sudden disappearance."

"In that case, my son, I wish you well in your journey to Yaoundé. Thank you for coming to explain your situation to me. If you'd gone to Yaoundé without my knowing why you left so suddenly without completing my daughter's bride price, I'd have given your disappearance a completely different interpretation."

Akuma stood up. "I should be going now, Pa. I have so much to do before my departure."

"It was a worthwhile visit," Pa Watechi said. "A lot of things have been clarified in my mind now about you. I thank *Nwi* for that."

Akuma left Pa Watechi's compound and went straight to

Fabian's house. Ever since Fabian learnt carpentry about 10 years ago, he had left their main compound and built his own house on a plot he bought near the main market. He got to Fabian's house around 4 PM in the evening. Fabian had not yet come back from his carpentry workshop. He sent a small boy, one of Fabian's neighbours, to tell Fabian that his brother was looking for him. After a while, the boy came back and said Fabian was locking the workshop and would soon be home.

Fabian came to the house within 15 minutes. As soon as he saw Akuma he said in jest, "Hey, what a surprise visit. What brings the teacher to the carpenter's house? Just a minute, let me get the key and open the front door." He fumbled in his pocket, brought out a single key and opened the front door. "Come in Akuma. Sit down anywhere, it's your house." Akuma sat down on a small chair.

"How are things?" Fabian asked him.

"Nothing seems to be moving. My life seems to have come to a standstill."

"What do you mean?"

"I was at the Fon's palace today with the *Kwifor*. Father's death has to be celebrated before I am initiated into the *Kwifor*. They would require six goats, ten chickens, four drums of palm oil, six jugs of palm wine, and 20 crates of beer."

"So many things?" Fabian asked.

"That's not all. I went to Pa Watechi's compound after I left the Fon's palace."

"Was Sirra there?"

"She wasn't. But her younger sister, Beri, and her mother were in the compound. I didn't see their mother, but I ate some good corn *fufu* and *njama-njama* with Pa Watechi that was prepared by Sirra. It was after we had eaten that he told me Father didn't finish paying all the money for Sirra's *knock-door* and bride price."

"What! How much is left?"

"One hundred and fifty thousand francs. I still have to provide two tins of palm oil to his brothers and half-sisters."

"Where are you going to get the money to buy these things? Your salary and arrears in the Ministry of Finance have not yet been processed."

"That's why I came to see you," Akuma said. "I must go to Yaoundé and find out what's happening to my file. Without my salary and arrears, we'll be unable to meet the expenses of our father's *cry-die*. I want you to lend me some money for me to travel to Yaoundé and find out what has happened to my file."

"How much money do you need? How long do you intend to stay in Yaoundé?"

"Let's say about three weeks. It shouldn't take more than two weeks to find out what has happened to my file."

"Where would you stay? How would you eat? We don't have relatives in Yaoundé that I know."

"Listen, Fabian, you have more questions than I can provide answers. Father used to mention a certain Solomon Kimeng, his cousin, who went to Yaoundé several years ago. I'll look for him. Give me whatever money you have, whatever can take me to Yaoundé and back. I'll refund you the money when I come back."

"When do you intend to travel?"

"Wednesday, next week. It's a good day to travel. Everyone will be in the farms. Mother will not know I've left."

"You won't tell her you're travelling?"

"I don't intend to. She'll just notice that I'm not in the compound. You should only let her know I have travelled to Yaoundé after my departure."

"Why?"

"I don't know. I think she's gone through so much pain, particularly after the death of our father. She'll not want to lose her only son to an unknown, distant city. She'll prevent me from going to Yaoundé. You know how unwavering she can be when she makes up her mind on something."

"I'll see what I can do. Come and see me next week on Tuesday evening, say about 4:30 PM. I'll give you the money." Akuma stood up. "Won't you wait till I prepare something for us to eat?" Fabian asked.

"No. It will take a long time. Besides, I don't trust your cooking. We'll talk about your prospects of getting married when I return from Yaoundé." Akuma stepped out of the house and headed in the direction of their compound.

The following week on Tuesday, Akuma walked down past the main market to Fabian's house. Fabian's front door was open. Akuma knocked on the door before he walked into the living room. He found Fabian in the living room.

"Come into the bedroom," Fabian said.

Akuma followed Fabian into the bedroom, with Fabian leading the way. There was one chair and a small stool in the room. Fabian asked Akuma to sit down. As soon as Akuma sat down, Fabian removed the white sheet from the bed, leaving the bare mattress and the pillow.

"What are you doing?" Akuma asked him.

"I'm looking for a small box." He lifted the mattress as he spoke and pulled it sideways, letting it lean on the wall. He went down on his knees, looked under the wooden framework that supported the mattress and stretched his left hand under the bed. Moments later, he brought out a small wooden box from underneath the bed. He wiped his knees, stood up, and sat on a small stool in the middle of the room.

"What's in the box?"

"You'll soon know." He removed a small key from his left trouser pocket and opened the small lock that was on the box. Akuma stood up from his chair and came to where Fabian was sitting. Fabian removed the lock and lifted the lid open. Akuma looked into the box. It was stuffed with bank notes of all denominations from five hundred francs to ten thousand francs. Fabian dumped all the notes on the floor. "Come on, help me count them."

Some notes were twisted. Others were folded. There were both old and new notes in the big pile. The two brothers picked up the notes and began sorting them out into five hundred, one thousand, two thousand, five thousand, and ten thousand denominations. After they sorted them, they began counting the money. In less than ten minutes they finished counting and placed them on two neat piles on the floor.

"How much do you have in your pile?" Fabian asked.

"Sixty-five thousand francs."

"And yours?"

"Ninety thousand," Akuma said.

"That makes a hundred and fifty five thousand francs in total."

"That's a lot of money," Akuma said.

"My savings for the past three years."

"How much will you give me?"

"All of it. The entire one hundred and fifty five thousand." He put the two piles together and gave the money to Akuma.

"No," Akuma said. "You should keep some—"

"Take it. It's a long journey. You need it. We don't know how long you'll be in Yaoundé, the things you will do, what you'll eat. I know that you'll refund me the money when your arrears are paid."

"Thank you, Fabian."

"You don't have to thank me. It's for our father's honour and our family name. We all depend on you. What time do you intend to leave tomorrow?"

"I'll leave the compound before 5:30 AM. I don't want Mother or someone else to see me leaving. I want to take the first minibus to Bamenda."

"Good," Fabian said. "I'll meet you at the bus park at 6 AM." He gave Akuma a friendly tap on the shoulder as he stepped out of the house.

Fabian was at the bus park before 6 AM. He kept on looking

at his watch. The minibus was quickly filling up with passengers. There were only six more places left. Fabian glanced again at his watch. Ten minutes past six. Where was Akuma? At six-fifteen, he became alarmed. He was just about to go and look for Akuma when he saw him walking down the road in rapid strides. Akuma was out of breath by the time he reached the park.

"What happened?" Fabian asked him. "The bus is almost full. There're just three places left."

"It was your mother, Ma Yaje. My things were already packed and I was about to leave at five-thirty when I saw her. She just kept on moving up and down in the compound, in front of her house. I knew she would see me if I came out of the house with my travelling bag."

"She's an early riser," Fabian said, "even when I was still small. She rose early and did nothing in particular. Just going in and out of the house."

"She went into her house momentarily. It was already 6 AM. That's when I slipped out of the house and rushed down to the park."

"Get into the bus," Fabian said. "There're only two places left." They embraced each other and Akuma went towards the minibus. Fabian followed him. "Have a safe trip, and may the spirit of our father and ancestors guide and protect you during the journey and throughout your stay in Yaoundé."

The bus conductor started yelling, "*Bamenda one man! Bamenda one man! Motor done full oh! Bamenda one man! Time for go! No waste my time! Motor done full! Moof money for pocket, pay your bus fare! Motor done full oh! Bamenda one man!*"

"Thank you, Fabian," Akuma said. "You've been so helpful." They shook hands as Akuma entered the bus. A few minutes later the driver started the bus and revved the engine.

A man in black trousers and a white lace jumper, wearing a red traditional cap, ran down the road shouting, "*Driver wait. I beg, driver, wait oh. I beg, wait for me. I de go for Bamenda. Driver wait, oh.*" He held a black attaché case in his right hand.

When the man came up to the bus, the conductor said, "*Yes, sah, where you de go?*"

"*Bamenda,*" the man said. "*I de go for Bamenda.*"

"*Motor done full,*" the bus conductor told the man. "*Next bus. You go enter na de next bus.*"

"*Squeeze me inside,*" the man pleaded. "*I get urgent business for Bamenda.*"

"*No sah, I no fit. Dat one na overload. Gendarme and police dem go take all we money for road.*"

"*I beg, conductor,*" the man pleaded. "*I go add one extra thousand for the regular fare.*"

"*Go talk for driver,*" the conductor said.

The man went to the driver's side of the bus, talked briefly with the driver and handed him three thousand francs. The driver raised his voice and shouted at the conductor. "*Make e enter! Squeezam anywhere!*"

The man came to the conductor's side and entered the bus.

The conductor banged the door shut and yelled at the driver, "*Oya, driver, we go! Motor done full!*" The driver started the bus, shifted to first gear, and eased the bus out of the park.

THREE

The seventy-sitter Amour Mezam bus entered Yaoundé at 2:10 PM. Akuma was exhausted. A middle-aged woman who sat next to him, who had been to Yaoundé several times, asked Akuma whether he had been to Yaoundé before.

"No," Akuma said, "this is my first time."

She began pointing out the major landmarks to him, gesticulating her hands left and right, as the bus made its way towards Tongolo, the first stop where passengers would come out. "We're now in Etoudi," she said. "That's Unity Palace, over there, to the right. That's where the head of state lives. The flag on top of the building is lowered. That means he's out of the country."

As the bus approached Tongolo the woman turned and looked at Akuma. "Where in Yaoundé will you be staying?"

"I don't know."

"Do you have family here in Yaoundé?"

"Yes, my father's cousin," Akuma told the woman. "I've never met him. I don't know what he looks like or where he stays."

"Hmm, that's a difficult one," the woman said. "Are you carrying any money on you?"

"Yes."

"How much?"

"A lot. More than a hundred thousand."

The woman whistled. "You'll be robbed or killed by bandits if you're not careful. The best advice I'll give you is to go straight to CRTV radio, as soon as the bus gets to Biyem-Assi, and make a radio announcement. Provide family details about yourself and your hometown, and write your relative's full names in the announcement. I'll show you the radio house when we get to central town. Stay in the radio house until your relative comes and picks you up. Don't go anywhere else. Yaoundé is not safe for people like you who come here for the first time."

After the bus left Tongolo the woman continued. "That's the CRTV television house on your right. Can you see that wonderful building up there on the hill? That's *Mont Fébé* hotel. We're already at the Longkak roundabout. We're now going through the tunnel. That's the Ministry of Foreign of Affairs to your right. The City Hall is on that road to the left over there. It's a beautiful place. Okay, this is the radio house to your right. When you come out at Biyem-Assi, stop a taxi and simply say, *La Radio*. The taxi will bring you here."

"That's the Hilton, over there to your left. That other tall building is The Ministry of Higher Education. You see the star building to your left? That's the Prime Minister's office. We're now at the Ministries. That's the Ministry of Secondary Education. P&T is over there. And that's Finance. The Public Service is to your left, on the same side with the Ministry of Transport. That's Mines Water and Energy to your left." The woman continued her running commentary until the bus got to Biyem-Assi.

Akuma came out of the bus holding the bag. He took a taxi to the broadcasting house as the woman had advised him. When he finished writing the announcement and paid for it, the woman at the reception told him the Luncheon Date announcements will be read after the 3 PM English news. She showed him a room in which lost people and strangers waiting for their relatives spent their time.

Akuma heard the 3:30 PM Luncheon Date announcements in the radio of one of the security guards at the radio station. He was appealing to Solomon Kimeng, a cousin of Fontamo Njebufah in

Menamo, to come and pick up Akuma, son of the same Fontamo Njebufah, from the broadcasting house. He waited till 6 PM, but no one came to look for him. The guard told him that he would have to sleep in the waiting room until his relative came. If he was hungry and wanted to eat something he could cross the road and buy some food in a cheap local eating house.

The next day passed and no one came to look for him at the broadcasting house. Akuma became worried when the guard told him they won't tolerate him in the waiting room beyond three days.

On the third day, when nobody came for him by 1 PM, he became very anxious. What would he do now? Where would he stay? Should he go directly to the Public Service, to Finance or to the Prime Minister's office? It was 4 PM as he sat on the bench in the waiting room thinking about the awkward situation he had found himself when he heard the guard yell, "*Monsieur* Akuma! *Monsieur* Akuma!"

Akuma came out of the waiting room and saw a man in his late 40s standing next to the guard. The man's body was emaciated and he had a rough beard and puffy exhausted eyes set upon a dark sullen face. Akuma walked straight to the man. A voice within him told him that this was Solomon Kimeng, his father's lost cousin in Yaoundé.

"Uncle Kimeng?" he asked in a matter of fact voice.

"Yes," the man responded without any expression on his face. "Are you Akuma? Are you the one who made that Luncheon Date announcement about me?"

"Yes, Uncle Kimeng. I did."

"Now, listen, don't call me Uncle Kimeng. I'm not an old man. Call me Solomon or Solo. That's what they call me in Yaoundé. Come on, let's go." Akuma went to the waiting room and took his bag. He thanked the guard as they left the broadcasting house and walked out to the road.

An empty taxi came and Kimeng said, "*Cent cent, deux places.*

Chapelle Obili."

The taxi driver honked once.

"Enter," Kimeng said.

It was past four when they got to his small one-bedroom house next to the bakery at Chapelle Obili. "This is where I stay," Kimeng told Akuma. "I'm still renting. I live here alone. I have no wife, no children. As you can see, I have two chairs, a small bed and an additional mattress in the bedroom."

"How much do you pay for this place?" Akuma asked him.

"It used to be fifteen thousand a month. Now it's twenty-five thousand every month. It's become so expensive. I'm looking for a cheaper place. How long will you stay here with me?"

"I don't know," Akuma said.

"Why? What have you come to do in Yaoundé?"

"I've come to follow my salary and arrears at the Ministry of Finance."

"Your salary? You have a job?"

"Yes. I graduated from the Teachers' Training College."

"Oh, so you're a teacher?"

"Yes. I was sent to teach at the Government Secondary School in Meghani, a small town next to our village."

"Well," Kimeng said, "we'll manage in this place while you're here. You'll sleep on the mattress in the parlour."

"That will be fine with me. Uncle Ki ... sorry, Solo. What do you do in Yaoundé?"

"Well, nothing in particular. Mostly odd jobs. I studied building construction, but I'm also a house electrician. I can't stay for two weeks without getting a job in the several construction sites dotted across the city. That's how I manage to survive. It keeps me going."

It was getting to 6 PM and Akuma was very hungry. "I'm very hungry," he told Kimeng. "I've had nothing to eat the whole day."

"There's no food in the house. I don't have a kitchen or plates.

I eat mostly street food. There's a zinc bathroom behind the house where all tenants bathe with buckets. The blue plastic bucket over there is for drinking water. The pink one in my room is for bathing. We hardly have water here. Occasionally it comes at night after 2 AM. There's a gutter at the back, next to the veranda, where you can brush your teeth."

"Well, in that case, let's go out and eat something."

"We?" Kimeng asked. "I'm short on cash. I expect to be paid tomorrow for a construction job I did at Mendong."

"You can't remain hungry like that!"

"Oh, I'm used to it," Kimeng said. "I sometimes stay for two days without eating."

"Two days!"

"Yes. I only drink water. It's not easy living in Yaoundé. Most people eat but once a day."

"What can one eat in the street?"

"Mostly roast fish, pork, and *suya*," Kimeng said, "with a choice of *bobolo* or fried ripe plantains."

"Well, let's go out and eat something. I'll pay for both of us."

"There's a good place down the street from the bakery. An Ewondo woman there makes very good fish." Kimeng locked the door with his key as they came out and went down the street for their evening meal.

The following day was a Saturday. When Akuma woke up and looked at his watch, he was surprised that it was already past 9 AM. He had not realized how tired he had been the previous evening. He carried the mattress into Kimeng's room and was surprised that Kimeng had already left the house. He came back to the living room and discovered that the front door wasn't locked. He stayed in the house the whole day, waiting for Kimeng.

At about three in the afternoon, he went to the bakery, bought bread and a tin of sardine. He came back to the house, opened the sardine tin and made himself a sandwich. He ate the sandwich, drank a cup of water and sat down in the house, waiting for Kimeng.

Kimeng came back at 6 PM. As soon as he entered the house, Akuma said, "Where did you go to Solo? I've waited for you all day."

"To Mendong," Kimeng said. "I told you so yesterday."

"Did they pay you?"

"Yes," Kimeng said. "Forty-five thousand francs. Here, take this."

"What's it?"

"A duplicate key. I made it for you in Mendong. You need it to enable you come and go as you wish."

"Have you eaten anything?" he asked Kimeng.

"Yes. Some beans and *beignet*. In Mendong. Come and take the mattress. I'm going to sleep right away. See you in the morning."

Akuma took the mattress and lay down. He tried to sleep but couldn't. His mind went back to his hometown, to Fabian, who had lent him the money to come to Yaoundé; to his mother and stepmothers; to Sirra and to Pa Watechi; to the discussion he had with the Fon and members of the *Kwifor* secret society. He did not know when he fell asleep.

When he woke up at 6:30, Kimeng was gone. He brushed his teeth, washed his face before he went out to the street. He saw a group of people gathered in a roadside shack further down the road. When he got there, he realized they were all male, standing and surrounding a woman who was selling pap and puff balls. He stood there for a while, listening, watching, and observing. The woman's name was Mami Pascal. She spoke Pidgin English to the men as she served them. After about ten minutes, Akuma went back to the house, took a five hundred francs coin and came back to the place. He heard a man call the puff balls *beignet*, in French. Another man said, "*bouillon de deux cents* and Mami Pascal gave him two generous servings of the pap.

He walked up to Mami Pascal, handed her the five hundred francs coin and said, "*Beigne*t for one hundred and *bouillon* for two hundred francs."

Mami Pascal looked at him before she served him a bowl of hot pap and eight puff balls on a flat plate. She glanced at him again and said, "*You be stranger for Yawindê?*"

"Yes," Akuma said.

"*You commot which place for Bamenda?*" she asked, giving him his three hundred francs change.

"Menamo," he said. "I'm from Menamo."

"*I be Barforchu woman. My man commot for Babanki. You de stay for whosai?*"

"Up the road," Akuma said. "With my uncle."

"*Cam chop beignet and drink pap here every morning. All man pikin dem de chop na for here.*"

"Thank you, Mami Pascal." After he finished eating Akuma went back to the house. He waited for Kimeng all day. At 10 PM he locked the door with the key, put the mattress on the floor, and slept.

The next day Kimeng was nowhere to be seen. Akuma became alarmed. Had he been hit by a car? Was he alive or dead? Where would he start looking for him? He knew no one in Yaoundé. He knew no police station, not even where the hospitals were located for him to start looking for Kimeng. That night, before he slept, he prayed to God to bring Kimeng back home safely.

The next morning, just when he was about to get up, he heard the key turn in the lock. Kimeng came in. There was mud on his shoes. He went out again, left the shoes outside before he entered the house with his bare feet.

Akuma jumped up from the mattress. "What happened to you? Where have you been these two days?"

"I gave you a key, didn't I? To allow you go in and out of the house as you wish."

"So that you can disappear for two days?"

"Why not?"

"If you don't see me in the house for a day or two, won't you get worried?"

"Why should I? What's there to worry about?" He came up to Akuma. He was drunk and dishevelled. Beer and whisky reeked from his breath. "You're a handsome young man. This is a big city with lots of lonely women who would harbour you in their houses, feed you, buy you clothes—expensive shirts, suits, nice ties. Come on village boy, why should I be worried if you disappear and fool around with some beautiful woman for a day or two?" He laughed loudly as he walked into his room.

On Monday morning, Akuma took a taxi and came out where the talkative woman had told him most of the ministries were located. He was fortunate to meet a man from Ekondo Titi who told him that the search for salary arrears actually began from the Ministry of Public Service, not the Ministry of Finance as he had thought

FOUR

The pensioner heaved a very long sigh. "So this is how you came to Yaoundé."

"Yes. When I got here, I didn't have time to appreciate the wonder of what I had heard was a city with tall buildings, beautiful women, and an alluring night life. It was later, much later, after my accident that I came to know its sordid and foul character."

"Your accident? What accident?"

"The one that paralysed me, that turned me into a disabled man."

"You mean ... you ... you weren't born like this? You weren't like this before?"

The disabled man became indignant. He pushed the wheelchair furiously from behind the table and came to the middle of the container.

"For two whole weeks, no one could trace my file at the Public Service. It was in the third week of my stay in Yaoundé that someone in the Ministry told me I had to give twenty-five thousand francs to resurrect my file from whatever drawer it laid entombed for six months. I had no choice. My father's *cry-die* was a priority. My inheriting his position as notable and kingmaker in the palace were also at stake. It was in the afternoon of a Wednesday, I think, that I began climbing the stairs to go up the eighth floor to see a certain director with the envelope I had prepared. The elevators had broken down several weeks before, of course. It was a tiring ascent, moving up the winding staircase. It was on that

Wednesday afternoon that I ... I ..." his voice wavered. His lips began trembling. He turned the wheelchair slowly and faced the opposite wall of the container.

"What happened?"

He remained silent for about a minute, then he turned the wheelchair round. He wiped away what appeared to be drops of tears from his eyes. He stared at the ceiling for a moment or two before he glanced at the pensioner.

"This is what is left of me." He looked at his withered legs. "This is what I've become." In a matter-of-fact voice, he said, "I fell down the stairs."

"Good God!"

"There weren't a lot of people on the staircase. It was in the late afternoon. I wanted to take advantage of that time. The director was waiting for me. He told me he would stay in his office later than usual. I was going up the fifth floor when my knees suddenly became weak and my entire body collapsed. I had not had a proper meal for three days. Perhaps it was the heat, the hunger and fatigue, I don't know. I lost consciousness as I rolled down the stairs.

"When I regained consciousness, I found myself in a hospital bed. It took me a while to recognize where I was. With the help of the nurses and the doctor who was in charge of my case, I came to know what had happened. After the fall, I was in a coma for two weeks. As the nurse spoke, I felt numbness below my waist. I pulled off the white sheet that covered my body. That was when I knew what had really happened. I was paralysed. I had lost the use of my lower limbs. I knew, at that moment, that I would never walk again."

"What a terrible thing! What a terrible thing!" the pensioner kept on repeating to himself.

"I was devastated. You can imagine how I felt. I went into a deep depression for about three weeks. Then I was thrown out of the hospital because I couldn't pay the medical bills. I tried to recall events, to remember things, to find out who I was. I couldn't. I had lost a greater portion of my memory. I roamed the streets alone, begging for food and money, creeping along unfamiliar alleyways, holding up my begging bowl to benevolent shoppers in front of supermarkets, banks, nightclubs, bars … I don't know how I survived the first three months. Gradually my memory returned. I remembered who I was, where I came from—my mother, my stepmothers, my half-brother, my teaching job, my late father's funeral celebration. For the first time, the immensity of this city pierced my heart with a thousand arrows."

"You didn't go back?"

"How could I? The only possession I had on me was my national identity card. How could I go home? Where would I start my narrative? How would I explain what had happened to me? It was then that the thought of hanging myself, letting it all end, came to my mind. I got a strong cord and located an unfinished building. I managed to attach the long rope to one of the beams in the building and passed the noose over my neck. I was just about kicking the big stone that supported my weight under me when memories of the dream came flooding into my mind."

"What dream? What are you talking about?" The pensioner had been so fascinated by the story that his mouth hung open throughout the man's narrative.

"While my body lay imprisoned in the hospital bed and my brain lay in comatose, the real me roamed around. I found myself in strange lands, in places I hadn't known existed beyond the physical realm. I don't know whether I should call them dreams. Can one dream continuously for two weeks? No, they were visions. Journeys into the spiritual worlds of God. In one of these journeys, I found myself on a vast, endless road. I don't know for how long I walked on the road. Oh, how can I describe the scenery? I kept on walking. It seemed like a journey without end. Then I came upon an enormous sparkling river. A long arched bridge spanned the length of that wonderful river. I stepped on the bridge and commenced crossing the river. Through a mist that was rapidly solidifying into a fog, I observed a city with bright lights at the other end, on the river bank. There was something mysteriously inviting about the city, the lights, and the fog. I knew I would not come back if I crossed that bridge.

"I was half-way across the bridge when I saw an unusual shape emerge from the fog on the other side of the bridge. As the distance between us diminished, the shape actually took form. It was a thin lanky man riding a black stallion. When we met in the middle of the bridge, he descended from the horse. He had a weather-beaten face and peculiar eyes that bore into my being like hot coals. He wore a dark robe with brown sandals. He wore nothing else. He also held a long staff that was made of a strange wood I had never seen before. A pleasant aura of light appeared to surround his being. Standing near him gave me the most pleasant feeling I had ever felt. He bowed slightly as he greeted me. He had a blunt straightforward manner about him.

"You can't come further than this," he said. "You must go back."

"I tried to argue, but he was adamant. Then I started to cry. I told him I was lost and didn't know who I was and that I wanted to go to the city of lights across the bridge. But he stood firm."

"You have to go back," he insisted.

"There was no use arguing with him. As I turned to go, he called me by my name. I turned round. He walked up to me and handed me the staff. He said, "Take this. You'll find it useful when you return." As he handed me the staff a strange sensation, like an electric current ran through my entire being. I heard the nurses say afterwards that when I regained consciousness, my right hand was folded into a fist as if I was clinging on to something, something I didn't want to let go.

"As I recollected this dream, the thought of killing myself

quickly left my mind. Something beyond human comprehension had happened to me. It didn't take long before I discovered what it was. I had been endowed with unusual supernatural powers beyond the comprehension of mortal minds."

"And what about your hometown, where you came from?"

"It's now a distant memory. What matters to me is now, being here. What I do for a living."

"At least, you could have sent a letter to your mother, your brother, the carpenter, or to Sirra, the girl you intended to marry? You loved her, didn't you?"

"I don't know. Love doesn't exist in my vocabulary anymore. Not with what I've gone through in this city. I do what I have to do. Nothing more, nothing less."

"But you could let your family know you're alive and well," the pensioner tried to persuade him.

"Alive? Who, me?" A cynical grin appeared momentarily on his face. "I died a long time ago. Nobody comes to Yaoundé and goes back alive. Those who manage to return go back half-dead. You may go back physically. Yes. But part of you remains here, forever."

"Apart from ... well ... what the sign-board outside says, is this all you do?" the pensioner wondered, "telling people's fortunes? Seeing into their future?"

"Isn't it sufficient to keep oneself alive?"

"I didn't mean to offend you," the pensioner apologised.

"I do several other things."

"Like what?"

"It depends. People come here to ask for all kinds of favours."

"Favours?"

"Yes. Students, housewives, directors, ministers. Some want quick promotions. Others appointments. Women want charms to keep their husbands at home. Students want certificates. The GCE or the BAC."

"Certificates? I don't understand. One needs to write exams, to pass."

"And what about those who can't pass? Those who have tried several times and failed? Of course, they come here."

"But—"

"Anything is possible in this country," Akuma said sarcastically. "It all depends on the right contacts, who you know."

"I see," the pensioner nodded. He stole a glance at his watch.

"What time is it?" the disabled man asked him.

"It's almost 7:30 PM. I didn't realise the time has gone by so quickly." He stood up. "I live with my paternal nephew. He'll get worried if he doesn't see me after nightfall."

"How far away is his house?" the disabled man asked.

"Quite a distance from here."

"In that case, someone will have to accompany you. The streets are not safe after seven."

The disabled man rolled the wheelchair towards the door and tapped the wall of the container twice. The pensioner heard footsteps outside. A man opened the door and pushed his face through.

"Yes, *Général*," the man said.

"Take this man safely to where he stays. He lives some distance away from here. Make sure nothing happens to him."

"As you say, *Général*," the man replied before his head disappeared out of sight.

"One of my men," the disabled man explained. "He's waiting outside. He'll take you home safely." The pensioner moved towards the door.

"One more thing before you leave," the disabled man said. "I know some influential people at the Ministry of Public Service. I'll get them to see into the problem of your file."

"They were quite certain my old file is lost. They asked me to come tomorrow morning and put together a new file."

"Just go ahead and do whatever they tell you. I'll use my own channels to keep track of your file. And do pass by tomorrow evening to let me know your progress."

"I don't know how to thank you," the pensioner said, as he stretched his hand and shook hands with the disabled man.

The disabled man smiled. "Destiny sent you to me. I have a role to play in your life." He rapped the side of the container again. A man's face appeared on the door just as the pensioner began to go out.

"Before you go," the disabled man began. "I almost forgot." He thrust his hand into the pocket of his large shirt and brought out the five hundred and one hundred francs the pensioner had put into his begging bowl. "Here, have this."

"The change I gave you?"

"Yes. You'll need it."

The pensioner took the coins and dropped them in his bag. He thanked the disabled man and stepped out of the container. It was now quite dark outside. The shadowy form of the man outside held a lighted torchlight.

"Come with me," the man said. The pensioner followed the beam of the torch through the clearing along the narrow path that led back to the street. He took a furtive glimpse behind his shoulder. The container was no longer visible. It had disappeared into the enveloping darkness of the night.

* * *

The next day, the pensioner walked up to the Anguissa junction and stood with the rest of the people who were waiting for the minibuses and taxis. It was close to 8:30 AM when he boarded a taxi that was going towards the ministries. He sat at the back with three other men.

He came out of the taxi in front of the Ministry of Education. He looked left and right before crossing the street. He went through the ground floor of the ministry and came out on a narrow passage that separated the Ministry of Education from the Ministry of Public Service. Hawkers were selling cigarettes, biscuits, sweets, pens, pencils, magazines, and newspapers. Several young men had mobile photocopy services between the two ministries. The pensioner walked round the back of the Ministry of Public Service and entered the building through the entrance facing the Central Lake. He climbed the stairs slowly and came up to the second floor. He rested for a while to catch his breath before he walked down the narrow corridor to Room 219B. The door was ajar, but he still knocked before he walked in.

It was a small room with three people in it. A thin elderly woman was peering at a flat monitor as she typed a document. She looked up as the pensioner entered the room. A man sat at a small table opposite her. He seemed to have fallen asleep over the table. Another man behind a table near the door was reading a newspaper. He hardly looked up as the pensioner entered the room.

"*Oui,*" the woman said in French, "what do you want?" Her question and tone were brusque and hostile.

The pensioner tried to respond in the limited French he knew. "I was..." he hesitated. "Someone told me yesterday to come to this room and begin the process of my pension dossier all over," he said.

"It's Pierre you have to talk to. That's his job," she said, pointing to the sleeping man. She resumed typing.

The pensioner stood there fumbling with the lapel of his jacket and the bag around his shoulder. The woman did not look up again from what she was typing. The man whose face was hidden behind the newspaper was still busy reading. The other man began to snore. It was more than five minutes since the pensioner had walked into the room. His legs began hurting.

"I'm sorry," he began, "I can't wait forever. This is my second week here. I've already—"

"Pierre! Pierre!" the woman called. She stopped typing momentarily. The sleeping man woke up with a start. "Did you have a sleepless night last night or what? You should be ashamed of yourself. You have a client waiting for you."

The sleeping man shook his head and robbed his eyes. "*Mon Dieu*, Annette, you disturb me a lot. Why can't you leave me alone?"

"I say, you have a client."

The sleeping man turned his head toward the door. His eyes were red from lack of sleep. He looked at the pensioner and said, "*Oui, Monsieur*, what can I do for you?"

"I'm a retired man," the pensioner said in broken French. "I have to compile a new dossier."

"What service? How many years?"

The pensioner hesitated. He didn't understand what the man meant.

"What department were you in the civil service? And for how long? Don't waste my time, *Monsieur*."

"Yes, yes. I understand. Thirty-five years. I was a principal. First a head teacher, and later on a principal. For thirty-five years."

"I don't like principals," the man who had been reading the newspaper spoke for the first time, lowering the paper. The sleeping man and the woman laughed. The pensioner looked perplexed.

"It's a joke," the sleeping man said. "One of his jokes. And for how long have you been retired without a pension, *Monsieur*?"

"Seven years."

"Seven years! But that's not possible. What have you been doing all these years?"

"My file is stuck in this ministry. They say it's missing. I have to start all over again, to compile a new file."

"And do you know what documents you need for the dossier?" the sleeping man asked.

"I can't remember," the pensioner said.

The sleeping man pulled out a sheet of paper from a drawer. He wrote down *Composition du dossier* and underlined it. He wrote a list under it.

- *Demande timbrée a 1000 FCFA*
- *Copie Acte de marriage*
- *Copie Acte de Naissance des enfants mineurs*
- *Certificat de vie collectif des enfants mineurs*
- *Certificat de scolarité des enfants mineurs*
- *Certificat de domicile*
- *Bulletin de Solde*

He took the paper from the table and handed it to the pensioner. "*Voilà*," he said. "We need all these documents."

The old man looked at the list. He scratched his head and looked at the man who had given him the paper. He tried to say something but hesitated.

"*Oui, Monsieur. Qu'est-ce qu'il y a encore?*"

"I didn't anticipate my file will get lost. My marriage certificate, the birth and school certificates of my teenage children, this *certificat de domicile*—all these things. The only thing I have on me is an old pay voucher and my national identity card. I don't know where I'll get the rest of the documents."

"*Ah, mon Dieu! Mais vous les anglophones. Vous dérangez trop,*" the woman exclaimed, throwing her hands up in the air in a gesture of total exasperation.

The old man became angry. "It's not my fault that this country is the way it is. You better be careful how you talk to me," he shouted. "I served this nation for almost half of my life, with all dedication." He raised his hand in a threatening gesture and moved towards the woman. The sleeping man jumped up and stepped between the pensioner and the woman who was now cowering against the wall. There was fear on her face.

"*S'il vous plaît, Monsieur,*" the sleeping man pleaded, still standing between the pensioner and the woman. "You must forgive her.

She does not know what she's saying." The man who had been reading the paper stood up. They both tried to restrain the old man. The pensioner put down his hand, turned round suddenly, and walked out of the room.

He walked quickly along the corridor and came to the lobby. Then he began climbing the stairs. The stairs slowed him down a bit. Eventually, he alighted on the third floor and walked straight to Room 325. He didn't even care to knock before he pushed the door open and stepped into the room. It was a large office space that contained five clerks. Kimbu sat behind a table at the far end of the room when he walked in. He walked straight to his table.

"You know what's happened to me downstairs in Room 219B? How can they do this to me? How can I begin putting together a new file all over again, after all these years?"

"But that's what I told you yesterday," Kimbu said, as he looked at the old man. "You have to compile a new file. We can't trace the old one. We don't know in which section of the service it got lost. Please, sit down. Losing your temper in this place won't help you much."

The pensioner sat down on a chair. He was breathing heavily. 'I don't know what to do, where to begin."

"Well," Kimbu said, "did they give you a list?"

"Yes, here it is." He gave the paper to Kimbu. "I haven't got most of the documents with me. I didn't bring them. I thought my file was—"

"Forget about the old file. Do you have a cell phone network in your hometown?"

"No," the old man said.

"In that case, you have to go to the Radio House before midday and ask them to make an urgent announcement to your relatives back at home. They'll read it after the 3 PM news. Someone will have to bring these documents to Bamenda and send them through any of the bus agencies whose buses come to Yaoundé."

"And what do I do after that?"

"You just have to wait until the documents arrive. Even after they get here and you put your file together, it has to make the usual route through the filthy entrails of this ministry. First, the dossier has to go to the *Bureau* for registration. After that, it is taken to the *Chef de Service-Adjoint*. When it leaves his office, it passes through the *Chef de Service* before it reaches the office of the *Sous-Directeur*. Then the *Directeur-Adjoint* looks at it to make sure everything in the dossier is in order before he passes it to his boss, the director. The dossier now leaves the director's office and finds its way to *Courrier*. The boys at *Courrier*, the mail room, eventually take it to *Contrôle Financier* where your arrears and monthly pension will be cross-checked and re-calculated. The *Courrier* is the worst place in this ministry. They hold people's dossiers in there for months, even years. That's where most files get lost."

"Can't someone do something about it?"

Kimbu laughed. "Do something about it? Change this system? Is that what you mean? You think the French did not have a reason for making it function this way? Even with your so called advanced multi-party democracy, what government do you think can change the system?"

"But something should be done about it."

Kimbu laughed again. "They can hardly cope with the rising crime wave in the country. What more of curbing corruption? Perhaps you and I could have made a difference. But who cares to listen? Does your voice matter in this country? Are you not a retired old *Anglofool* chasing a lost file in the stinking corridors of this ministry?"

"Our time is over," the pensioner reflected. There was regret and defeat in his voice. "But you, the young men. There must be hope."

"Hope? Years ago I used to have hope. But today, when I look around me I see no hope. Bribery and corruption, nepotism, embezzlement of state funds, and tribalism have intensified. It's a lost cause. I'm a mere clerk here, far from the corridors of power. My voice can't go beyond the confines of this room. It won't make any difference to those men down there at *Courrier* whether I exist or not."

The pensioner sighed.

"When your dossier leaves *Contrôle Financier*, it goes back again to *Courrier*. They're the ones who finally carry it to the eighth floor, to the minister, for the final signature, whenever they wish. It's after the minister's signature that the dossier is forwarded to the Ministry of Finance."

"And how long does all this take?" There was a note of despair in the pensioner's voice.

"Anywhere from five weeks to five years. It all depends on you."

"On me?"

"How much money have you got on you?" Kimbu asked the old man.

"Not much," the pensioner admitted. "I brought barely enough to enable me to survive the few weeks I anticipated spending in Yaoundé. But why?"

"I advise you to change ten or twenty thousand into five thousand francs notes. Poverty haunts everyone here. People must survive."

What Kimbu was inferring gradually dawned on the old man. He took another deep breath and sighed wearily. "I see," he said, "I see. You mean I have to give money to every person on whose desk my dossier falls on?"

A knowing, congratulatory smile spread across Kimbu's bearded face. "You learn fast. But it's the men at *Courrier* you have to be careful with. They usually demand more, sometimes up to twenty thousand francs! They're the ones you've got to handle with care. You can't afford to let your new file disappear again."

The pensioner looked at his watch. He stood up. "I think I

should get down to the Radio House before midday."

Kimbu stood up and walked out with the old man. They came out into the corridor. He saw him walk down the stairs to the second floor before he returned to his office.

The pensioner came out in front of the Ministry of Secondary Education. It was almost 11 AM. He crossed the street and waited. Soon a taxi came along and stopped in front of him.

"*La Radio*," he said.

The taxi driver honked the car horn once.

The pensioner got into the taxi and sat on the dilapidated upholstery of the car's backseat.

FIVE

Lucas Wango was transferred from the Ministry of Basic Education where he was a head teacher to the Ministry of Secondary Education. By government decree, he was appointed principal of the Government Bilingual High School Kumba. This appointment came after he acquired an M.Ed degree by correspondence from the University College London.

At fifty-two, he was one of only five elites with a Masters degree from his division. He had an intuition that he would rise within the administration if he affiliated himself with and promoted the ideology of the ruling party. That is how he came to attend rallies, campaigns, and other political activities that involved the party. He was aware that legislative elections were scheduled for August, but he didn't realize that the top echelon of the party's well-oiled political machinery had recognized his dedication to the party until the Senior Divisional Officer in Kumba, called him that Friday afternoon. He was in his house having dinner with his wife when his cell phone rang.

"Hello," he said, "who's on the line?"

"Etende Zanga," the voice at the other end said, "the S.D.O. Where are you? I want you to come to my office now."

"Yes, sir," he said when he realized that it was indeed the S.D.O.'s voice. "I'm coming right away, sir."

"Who is it?" his wife Matilda, asked him. "You haven't even finished eating your food."

"It's the S.D.O. He says I should meet him in his office

immediately." He stopped eating, went into his bedroom and changed into a suit and tie before putting on his black shoes. He always wore his suit to school during important state occasions and whenever National Pedagogic Inspectors from the ministry in Yaoundé visited schools in his division. He knew suits, particularly black suits, would distinguish him in the crowd. One never knew the criteria that the political hierarchy in Yaoundé used to select people for government appointments, but one of his tribes men who was a senator in Yaoundé had advised him to always wear good-looking suits that will make him stand out in a crowd. He could be spotted out at any moment by the important men from Yaoundé. He went to his bedroom, looked at himself in the mirror, adjusted the knot of his tie, looked at himself again, and felt satisfied. He came out of the bedroom and looked at his watch. He had only used five minutes to dress up. He was still hungry, but he barely glanced at the food on the table and his wife as he stepped out into the street.

It was not yet seven thirty and there were still a lot of motor bike taxis on the streets. He signalled one of the bikes. The bike slowed down and the bike-man looked at his suit. "Yes, sir. To where?"

"Fiango," Wango said. "To the S.D.O.'s office."

"Five hundred," the bike man said.

Wango knew the fare was two hundred francs. The man had added an additional three hundred francs because of the suit he wore. He climbed behind and adjusted himself as the bike took off towards the downtown area, in the direction of the administrative quarter.

Wango knocked on the S.D.O.'s office door and a voice told him to come in. He entered the office and saw Etende Zanga, the S.D.O. sitting behind his desk. There were three other men in the office. He shook hands with the S.D.O. and the three men. He recognized the first man. He was Hansel Ebako, Member of

Parliament for Meme North. He looked at the other two men again. He had never seen them before. Everyone in the S.D.O's office, including the S.D.O, wore a suit.

"Sit down Mr Wango," the S.D.O. said. "You know Mr Ebako, I'm sure. Let me go straightaway to why I've invited you to this meeting. Everything we discuss here is confidential and should never, I repeat never, be disclosed to the public. The gentleman to your right is *Monsieur* Mvodo. He's from the Presidency. The man to your left is *Monsieur* Ango Marcel. He's a member of our party's Central Committee. As the S.D.O. for this division, I've noted with satisfaction your active participation in party activities. For two years now, since your appointment as principal of the Government Bilingual High School, you've devoted yourself to the party. That's why we proposed to the political hierarchy in Yaoundé that your name be added to the party's Central Committee. Congratulations, *Monsieur*, Wango."

The first man, *Monsieur* Mvodo from the Presidency said, "Legislative elections are coming up next month. The opposition has a stronghold in your region. We need a courageous man like you to assist the party in breaking up the opposition stronghold in your constituency. The S.D.O. has suggested you can be trusted to carry out this delicate but important mission in—. Where does he come from?" Mvodo turned his head and looked at the S.D.O.

"Yambe," the S.D.O. said, "Mezam division."

"Yes, Yambe. We understand it's one of the biggest sub-divisions in Mezam."

"It is, *Monsieur*," Wango said.

Monsieur Ango, the Central Committee man said, "We have to win the vote in Yambe at all costs, *Monsieur* Wango. This is why the Central Committee, on behalf of our party, has delegated you to personally handle matters concerning the elections in Yambe."

Wango leaned forward. "What exactly am I supposed to do, *Monsieur* Ango? I'm not a member of ELEKAM, the electoral commission."

"Forget about ELEKAM," the S.D.O. said with disdain. "We've put into place our own machinery to win the elections in strategic constituencies all over the national territory."

"You'll leave for Yambe two weeks before the elections," the man from the Central Committee said. "When you get there, go straight to the Divisional Officer's house, not his office, you understand?"

"I understand, *Monsieur*."

"Don't go to the D.O.'s house in the day, only at night," *Monsieur* Ango continued. He stopped speaking and opened a black bag that was on the floor, next to him. He brought out an envelope and gave it to Wango. "Give the D.O. this envelope the same day you reach your hometown. It contains confidential information about your mission in Yambe." Wango took the envelope, looked at it for a brief moment before he put it in his inner coat pocket. "When you give him the envelope and he reads the letter, he'll tell you what to do."

Mvodo opened a brown diplomatic case next to him. "Your dedication to the party is very much appreciated." He brought out a large brown envelope and handed it to Wango. "Open the envelope and count the money in it so that the S.D.O. acknowledges that we didn't take a single franc from the money that is meant for you."

Wango took the envelope and opened it. It was full of bundles of crisp bank notes that had an odd, peculiar smell. There was silence in the room as he counted the money. When he finished counting the money he looked up and said in a shaky voice, "Five million francs." He could not recognise his own voice. He had never held so much money before in his entire life. His hand was shaking as he put the money back into the envelope and tucked it away into his coat pocket.

"Our national president insists on transparency and integrity in all party transactions," Mvodo said. He gave a form to Wango as he spoke. "Write today's date and sign your signature next to your name on the paper."

Wango took the paper and looked at it. It was a smooth, white, glossy letterhead from the presidency bearing the presidential seal and national coat of arms. There were several names on a list. He glanced down the page and saw his name. He signed his signature, wrote the date and gave the paper back to Mvodo.

"Well," Etende Zanga said, "the meeting is over. Let me remind you once more that this meeting never took place. Nobody, even your family members, should know why you came here. Tell them anything other than what we've discussed."

Wango stood up and was ready to go when Mvodo said, "Oh, I almost forgot. How could I? A week before you depart to Yambe, the S.D.O. will call you again. The party has allocated a brand new Toyota Land Cruiser and a driver to drive you to your hometown and back during the election period. We thank you very much, Comrade Wango. We shall recommend that you be given a medal after the elections."

The S.D.O., Hansel Ebako the MP, and the two men from Yaoundé stood up and shook hands with Wango as he went out of the office.

* * *

Wango could not believe that he was actually the one sitting on the owner's seat of an air-conditioned, chauffeur-driven Toyota Land Cruiser VX. Throughout the long drive to Yambe, he had pinched himself several times, wondering whether it was a dream, the kind of dream one suddenly awakens from to confront the drab habitual existence of daily life. Yes, it was true. He was actually the one, Lucas Wango, principal of Government Bilingual High School Kumba, in a brand new Toyota Land Cruiser, being driven by a chauffeur to his hometown. So this was what it meant to be a big man with money in your pocket—do anything you wanted to do, get any woman you fancied. He was so carried away with his thoughts that he did not realise they were already at the Oku-Yambe intersection.

"What side to take, *Monsieur*?" asked Belibi Alphonse, his French-speaking driver.

"Oh," he said, coming out of his reverie. "Left, turn left. The other road goes to Oku."

Belibi turned left in the direction to Yambe.

"You're a very careful driver, Belibi."

"Thank you, *Monsieur*."

Wango looked at the time on the dashboard. It was getting to 4 PM. "We'll get to Yambe in the next twenty-five minutes," he said to the driver. "We shall first go to my brother's compound. I'll greet him and his family before I get a room in the Guest Lodge. You'll sleep in my brother's house. There are several comfortable rooms there. The Guest Lodge is not far from his compound. We'll go to the D.O.'s house at 8 PM."

"*Oui, Monsieur*. Thank you."

When the car approached Yambe main market, Wango directed Belibi to his brother's house. Belibi drove slowly as he tried to avoid colliding with goats and pigs on the car's path. Wango asked him to stop in front of a large clearing in the middle of the compound. He came out of the car holding a black leather bag in which he kept his money. Two children, a boy and a girl, about five and eight years old, approached the car.

Wango came down from the car and the children greeted him politely in their native language. They did not seem to know him.

"I'm looking for Pa Gideon Wango. Is he your father?" he asked the children in their language.

"He's not at home," the girl said. "He's at the farm."

"What's he doing at the farm so late in the evening?"

"He went to harvest coffee. He will only come back at sunset," the boy said.

Wango had forgotten that this was the coffee season. "Tell him his brother from Kumba came to see him. I'm at the Guest Lodge. I'll come back again." He climbed back into the Land Cruiser and told Belibi to go back as they came. When they came out of the compound, he asked Belibi to drive down to the Guest Lodge which was just a stone's throw from his brother's compound.

Wango checked into a single room in the Guest Lodge while Belibi had a drink and watched satellite TV in the Lodge's bar. When he came out ten minutes later from his room, it was about six-thirty. He was just handing his key to the receptionist when his brother walked into the Lodge.

He exclaimed when he saw his brother. He raised his hands in the air, rushed forward and embraced him. "Gideon, you haven't changed a bit. Look at you."

"What do you mean I haven't changed," Gideon Wango said. "Look at me. Age and coffee farming have taken their toll on me. What brings you to Yambe? This is election time. I saw a Land Cruiser in front of the Lodge. Don't tell me it's my brother's Land Cruiser."

"It's mine, Gideon. I also have a government-paid driver who drove me from Kumba."

"*Hey, my broda, money fine oh*! Where did you get so much money?" Gideon asked.

Lucas laughed. "Top secret."

"Anything to do with the up-coming elections?"

"You're asking too many questions. Let's go to the restaurant. I'm hungry. I haven't eaten since I left Kumba I ate only plums and roast plantains in Kekem. We have so much to talk about, but we must first fill our stomachs."

"Which way is the restaurant?" Lucas asked the receptionist.

"That way, sir, to your right," the receptionist said.

"Thank you," Lucas said as he laughed loudly again at something his brother said.

* * *

It only took fifteen minutes for their food to be ready. As they ate, Lucas said, "Yes, you're right. I'm here because of the elections. You haven't changed parties, I hope."

"No, how can I? I've always listened to your advice. I'm still with the ruling party. He who has the yam and knife distributes the food."

"Good," Lucas said, "very good. "The elections are on Saturday. Today is Monday. I want you to be involved in whatever activities the D.O. will ask me to carry out here. There's a lot of money involved. I want you to arrange things and enjoy the benefits. After all, it's government money. I assure you, you'll have enough money to increase your coffee farms and production."

"Anything you say, brother, anything."

"First of all," Lucas went on, "I have to see the D.O.'s house tonight." He glanced at this watch. "It's only 6.45 PM. Belibi will drive me to the D.O.'s house at 8 PM."

"Belibi?" Gideon asked.

"Oh, I'm sorry. You haven't met my driver yet." He rang a bell in the restaurant and a waiter appeared promptly. "Tell the tall man who's drinking a beer in the bar to come and see me in the restaurant."

"Yes, sir."

A few minutes later, Belibi entered the restaurant. "You called me, *Monsieur*."

"Yes, Belibi. This is my elder brother. The one whose compound we went to when we arrived. We're blood brothers, from the same father."

"Good evening, *Monsieur*."

"Good evening," Gideon said. "Are you the one driving my brother?"

"*Oui, Monsieur*, it's me."

Lucas stuffed a piece of chicken in his mouth, chewed it ravenously before he looked up at Belibi. He glanced again at his watch. "Get ready. We'll soon go to the D.O.'s house. We'll drop my brother at his compound before we go to see him. When we come back you'll park the car in front of the Lodge and walk back to my brother's compound where you'll spend the night."

"It's a big compound," Gideon said. "I have two guest rooms and comfortable beds."

"Thank you, *Monsieur*."

"Okay, you can go now. We only have fifteen more minutes."

"*Oui, Monsieur*. Belibi is always ready. When you're ready, I am ready, *Monsieur*," Belibi said as he left the restaurant.

The Land Cruiser dropped Gideon at his compound before Lucas directed Belibi to the D.O.'s house near the Catholic Mission Health Centre. Wango waited in the car while Belibi rang the bell at the gate. Belibi could see lights in the house. He rang the bell a second time. The gate was opened from inside and a tall lanky man in a guard's uniform came out.

"A visitor to see the D.O.," Belibi said. Then he added, "An important visitor from the Central Committee in Yaoundé."

The uniformed guard saw the intimidating silhouette of the Land Cruiser in the darkness and said, "The visitor can come in. The D.O. is waiting for the 8.30 PM TV news."

Belibi went back to the Land Cruiser and told Wango that the gate was open and that the D.O. was in the house waiting for him.

Wango came out of the Land Cruiser and walked to the gate. He was wearing one of his best black suits. He had ensured that his shoes were well polished. He adjusted the knot of his tie and made sure his cuff links could be seen at the edge of his wrists. The guard bowed obsequiously as Wango walked in through the gate.

"This way, sir," the guard said, hastening forward and showing Wango the steps to the D.O.'s house. Wango barely glanced at the guard as he walked up the short staircase to the house.

The D.O. was on his feet as Wango stepped into the living room. "Egbe Tabi, from Mamfe," the D.O. said, introducing himself. "I've been waiting for you. Someone from the Central Committee in Yaoundé called to inform me you were on your way here."

"Delighted to meet you, D.O. Tabi," Wango said shaking hands with the D.O.

"Please have a seat. Can I get you something to drink? Martini, beer, brandy—"

"No, thanks."

"Angulu!" the D.O. yelled.

The uniformed guard entered the living room from a side door and said, "Yes, sah."

"Bring me a shot of brandy with ice."

"Yes, sah. Anything else?"

"That will do for now."

Wango reached into the pocket of his jacket and brought out the letter. He gave it to the D.O. before he sat down. Tabi sat down and read the letter. When he finished reading it he looked up.

"The Central Committee has sent you to assist me with elections in Yambe. They have absolute confidence in you."

The guard came in with the brandy and ice and put the drink on the table. Tabi said, "Thank you, Angulu. That will be all for now."

He took a sip of the brandy and said "I have a wife and three children—a girl and twin boys. The girl is nine and the boys are four. Whenever there are elections, I always send my wife and children to the village. Yambe is always volatile during elections. That's why the house is very quiet. I only have Angulu here to keep me company. Come, let me show you the delicate job the Central Committee has entrusted in our hands. Wango stood up and followed Tabi into a small room. There were ten transparent ballot boxes in the room. Tabi opened two big wooden boxes on the other side of the room. The boxes were loaded with prefabricated ballots containing the name of the man in Yambe who was running for elections to represent their party in Parliament.

"You've seen the ballots and the boxes yourself," Tabi said. 'Our party is still timid in Yambe. It doesn't have courageous men who'll distribute these ballots a day or two before the elections. They're scared of the opposition. As the D.O., I can keep the ballots in my home; but we need someone who is a Yambe native and speaks the local language to coordinate the distribution of the ballots and the ballot boxes to trusted militants of our party. That's why the Central Committee sent you here."

"Have you identified anyone in Yambe who can house the ghost polling stations?"

"As of now," Tabi said, "I only know of the Fon, the postmaster, and the principal of Government Bilingual High School Yambe."

"And my brother, Gideon and my paternal cousin, Francis. They're fearless. They'll be helpful in harbouring the ghost polling stations and distributing the ballots to our militants."

"That makes five people," Tabi said. "Two ballot boxes per ghost polling station. This is good news for the party."

"When would you want me to take the ballots and transparent ballot boxes?"

"Well," Tabi said, "a day or two before the elections on Saturday."

"I'll take them tonight," Wango said. "That will give me enough time to place the ballot boxes in their right places and make arrangements to distribute the ballots to our militants."

"Excellent! I'll call Angulu to help carry the boxes and ballot papers to your car. Angulu!" Tabi yelled again as they walked back to the living room.

Angulu appeared promptly and said, "Yes, sah."

"Go to that inner room, take the transparent boxes and the other two heavy boxes and bring them to the living room."

"My driver is in my Land Cruiser outside. Can he come in and help?"

"Certainly," Tabi said. "Four hands are better than two. Angulu, go out and call his driver. What's his name?"

"Belibi," Wango said.

"Ask Belibi to come in and help carry some material into Mr. Wango's car."

"Yes, sah."

A few minutes later, Angulu came in with Belibi. Wango said, "Belibi, there're 10 transparent boxes and two bigger and heavy boxes in a small room over there. You and Angulu will put them in the Land Cruiser."

"*Oui, Monsieur.*"

The two men went into the room and began carrying out the boxes. When they finished, Belibi went back to the car and Angulu went outside.

Wango looked at his watch. "It's almost 10:15 PM," he said as he stood up.

"It's going to be a very busy night for you," Tabi said as he suppressed a yawn. "It's almost bedtime for me." He walked down the short flight of stairs with Wango. "I don't envy you," he said. "From all indications, you'll be busy all night."

"I'll certainly be busy," Wango said. "I'll start at the Fon's palace right away before I move to the postmaster's house and the principal's house."

"I'll call them. They'll be waiting for you."

When they reached the gate, they shook hands. As Wango went out, Angulu shut the gate and locked it with two big padlocks. Tabi waited till the Land Cruiser started and drove away before he went up the stairs to his house.

* * *

Lucas Wango was having lunch the next day at the Guest Lodge when a waiter came in and told him a man wanted to see him. "Who's he? What does he want?" Wango asked the waiter.

"No idea sir. He says it's urgent. He must talk to you immediately."

"Well, bring him in."

"I'll do so right away."

A few minutes later a rugged-looking, diminutive man with red eyes entered the restaurant. Wango looked up as the man came in. His was emaciated and the scraggy beard on his face was dishevelled from lack of care. Wango had never seen the man before.

"Please sit down," he said to the man.

The man pulled a chair and sat down.

"I'll ring the bell and call one of the waiters," Wango said. "Let them get you a beer. Have a look at the menu and choose something for lunch. I'll foot the bill."

"Thank you," the man said in a hoarse, raucous voice. "Very kind of you. I've come here for another matter. I don't think we know each other," the man said. "I understand you're the principal of GBHS Kumba."

Wango looked surprised. "Yes, I am."

"Schools are still going on in Kumba, aren't they? What are you doing in Yambe?"

"And who the hell are you?" Wango asked the man.

"The divisional representative of the opposition SDA party in Yambe," the man said.

"I see," Wango said. He was becoming impatient with the man's intrusive and conceited mannerism. "And what, if I may ask, is this visit about?"

"I've come to warn you."

"Warn me? About what?"

"Our eyes and ears are everywhere," the man said. "You came to Yambe yesterday evening and visited the D.O. at about 8 PM. You left his house very late. Your driver didn't drop you at the Guest Lodge. You went to the Fon's palace, then left for the postmaster's and principal's houses. You left the principal's house way beyond midnight. The postmaster and the principal are not Yambe indigenes. What were you doing in the D.O.'s house?"

Wango kept quiet. The man from the opposition looked him steadily in the face.

"Something is amiss," the man warned Wango, "and they're trying to pull you into it. We'll find out what it is before Saturday. We know it's got to do with the upcoming elections. We don't know what it is, but it's something fishy. We can smell it, and it stinks. Don't get your hands soiled in other people's faeces. You'll only have yourself to blame." He stood up abruptly and walked out of the restaurant.

A few hours before dawn on Saturday, opposition vanguards raided the ghost polling stations in Yambe. They seized the stuffed ballot boxes and started marching to the D.O.'s office. Tabi heard the shouts and chants in his sleep. He got up, put on his bedroom light, and looked at the time on the walk clock. It was 5:15 AM. The commotion came from the vicinity of his administrative office. He was still in his pyjamas as he came out in the living room. He opened the front door. Angulu was fast asleep and snoring loudly in the garage.

"Angulu!" Tabi shouted

Angulu woke up with a start. "Yes, sah!"

"Can you hear the shouting and songs? What direction are they coming from?"

Angulu listened intently. As soon as he heard the commotion.

he turned to the D.O. and said, "Sah, the noise is coming in the direction of your office."

"Open the garage gate at once," Tabi ordered. "We have to go and find out what's going on."

Angulu opened the garage gate. The D.O. entered his Suzuki jeep, cranked the engine and pulled out of the garage. Angulu closed the gate, came out and entered the jeep with Tabi. They drove down the short distance to Tabi's office. The jeep's headlights illuminated a crowd of about fifty removing ballots from two boxes and throwing them in front of the D.O.'s office. As the jeep approached the office, someone in the crowd began pouring what appeared to be kerosene on the ballot papers.

"Matches," a voice shouted. "I need matches to set the ballots ablaze. Another man shouted, "Burn down the D.O.'s office. He's one of them. Burn it down."

The D.O. stopped the jeep and dialed the number of the gendarmerie legion commandant. When he heard the commandant's voice he said, "Commandant, it's the D.O. This is an emergency. A mob of opposition supporters is about to set fire to my office. Bring your men here at once! This is an emergency!"

The commandant said, "I've heard you D.O. I'll be there with my men in five minutes."

By the time the legion commandant arrived with a contingent of heavily armed men, the mob had already set the ballots ablaze. The fire was spreading rapidly to the D.O.'s office. A scuffle broke out between the mob and the heavily armed gendarmes. Shots and teargas were fired. The mob fought back with sticks and stones. When two unarmed men were shot and killed by the gendarmes, the mob was enraged. The mob left the D.O.'s office and headed for Gideon Wango's compound. When it reached the compound, the men broke down the doors of his house and ransacked it as they searched for the stuffed ballot papers. They went into a frenzy when they discovered the ballot papers and two ballot boxes in

Gideon's house. They dragged Gideon out and set the house on fire.

Belibi managed to escape from Gideon's compound at 5:45 AM. He ran down to the Guest Lodge and banged furiously on Wango's door. Wango got up at once, opened the door and came out.

"What's going on, Belibi?" Even before he finished asking the question he heard the uproar in the distance. More shots were fired.

"*C'est grave, Monsieur Wango! C'est très grave!* They coming here to the guest house. We go now. They scatter your brother's compound, set houses on fire. When he get up from sleep, they drag him out and ask where his brother from Kumba is staying. I fear, monsieur, I fear your brother's life."

Wango heard distant shouts and gun fire. The mob was certainly coming down to the Guest Lodge. There were more gun shots. "We get no time, *Monsieur*," Belibi cried. "They coming to Guest Lodge to look for you. We leave at once."

Wango ran back to his room and dressed hastily. He put the remaining money and carrier bag in the car. Belibi started the Land Cruiser, went into reverse, changed gears and moved the car forward facing the road to Bamenda. Wango got into the Land Cruiser and Belibi took off for Bamenda. It was after their escape to Bamenda, as they drove to Kumba, that Wango listened to the 1 PM news on the car radio and heard of the killings of civilians and gendarme officers in Yambe. When he got to Kumba he was horrified to learn that his brother and cousin to whom he had given ballots and boxes and two hundred and fifty thousand francs each had been lynched by the mob.

He quarrelled with Matilda concerning his involvement in what she called 'dirty politics' one Sunday afternoon. She said she could no longer bear the scorn and isolation in her women's cultural group. The women had refused her to host the Yambe women *njangi* meeting.

"You must resign from this Central Committee thing you've involved yourself in," she said.

"Resign from the Central Committee? Have you lost your mind? No one resigns from the Central Committee."

He went to his private office and came back shortly with a bundle of new bank notes. He threw them on the dinning table and shouted at her to count the money. She picked up the bundles of crisp bank notes and examined them one after the other.

"This is new money, a lot of money. How much is it?"

"Three and a half million francs," he said.

She was astonished and confused. "Three and a half million! So much money!" Her voice was now reduced to a mere whisper.

"My affiliation with the ruling party is an inevitable choice for our survival," he told her. "Do you think I hate my own people in Yambe? Am I happy to have lost my brother and cousin? Sometimes, in the early hours of the morning, when the nightmare of the horrifying deeds and actions I got involved in chase away sleep from my weary eyes, I ask myself, what I've done. Right now, I have no answers."

* * *

Three months after the legislative elections, when there were rumours of an imminent cabinet reshuffle, Etende Zanga called Wango to his office and introduced him to Atangana Messanga from the Presidency. Wango took the man out for lunch at the Azi Hotel and Resort. Atangana was so hungry that he wolfed down the delicious food quickly. *La nourriture est bonne ici, eh. Vraiment, mais vous les Anglophones, vous vivez bien ici à Kumba.* As they ate, Atangana opened a file and showed him a list of four elites who had been recommended for a ministerial appointment in his division. Atangana told him that a former Secretary of State in the Ministry of Public Service, a man from Yambe, will be dropped from the government in the next cabinet reshuffle. As compensation for his dedication to the party, the destruction of their family compound, and the death of his relatives, Wango was going to be appointed a minister.

"The head of state knows the tragedy that occurred in Yambe and the death of your brother and cousin. He has asked me to personally extend his condolences and solidarity to you." Atangana went on to say that he and a few close collaborators were in the inner circle that met, talked with, and advised the head of state on a regular basis.

"Is the head of state aware of the appalling poverty in other parts of the country?" Wango asked Atangana.

"Yes, he is," Atangana said. "It's true he cannot be at all places everywhere in the country. So we're his eyes and ears. We report back to him what the people say and what they want. And he acts."

Wango was not satisfied. "Fifty years after independence and re-unification," he went on, "there are no proper roads in the country. Most infrastructures are broken down. Does he really hear the cry of the people?"

There was a slight, perceptible trace of impatience and exasperation on Atangana's face. The muscles of his upper left face twitched momentarily. "Listen, *Monsieur* Wango, I agree with you. Yes, sometimes the head of state appears to be remote and far removed from the difficult life and reality of ordinary people. But I assure you that he knows what's going on. The machinery of government is painfully slow. But development does take place eventually. The state has limited resources, as you very well know. Let me assure you that I'll personally inform him of your concerns. You're a very intelligent man, *Monsieur* Wango. As an elite member of our party who cares about the people's welfare, your views will be heard in Yaoundé, I assure you. The head of state needs people like you. I've taken note of everything you've said."

When Atangana asked for three million francs so that he and

the other advisers of the head of state should keep an eye on his ministerial file, Wango was just too obliged. He took Atangana to his house, introduced him to Matilda and gave him three million francs after Matilda and himself had entertained him with expensive bottles of red wine.

Wango became worried and uneasy when he went to Yaoundé to follow his advancement file at the Ministry of Finance and, later on, went to the Presidency to look for Atangana. He showed his party and professional identity cards to the military men at the reception.

"Which Atangana do you wish to see, *Monsieur*?"

"Atangana Messanga," he said.

"We don't have an Atangana Messanga in the presidency, *Monsieur*," one of the military men said. "There's one Atangana Messanga who is a technical adviser in the Ministry of Higher Education. We don't know if he's the man you're looking for."

Wango went to the Ministry of Higher Education and found out it was not the Atangana Messanga who came to Kumba.

A week later, when he returned to Kumba, he was in his office at the Government Bilingual High School when the S.D.O. called and asked him to come to his office. The S.D.O. was excited when Wango reached his office.

"There's a phone call for you from the Presidency. I told the man it would take about ten minutes for you to get here. He said he'll call back in twenty minutes."

Thirty five minutes later the phone rang and the S.D.O answered it before he beckoned Wango to take the receiver. It was Atangana Messanga. He was very upset that Wango came to look for him at the Presidency without booking an appointment.

"Listen," he said, "why didn't you call to let me know you were coming?" Atangana asked. "Well, why did you want to see me?"

"I simply wanted to pay you a courtesy call and greet you," Wango said.

"Listen," he told Wango. "My collaborators and I are keeping our eyes on your file. Be patient. Everything will be fine. Just be ready to buy me a bottle of champagne when ministerial appointments are made."

The S.D.O. was amazed that Wango was well-connected at the Presidency. Wango was jubilant. The phone call from the Presidency kept his hopes of becoming a minister alive.

At the end of the month, when the cabinet reshuffle and appointments were announced during the 1 PM radio news, a certain Marcel Mbida, a man from the South region, a one-time principal of Lycée d'Ebolowa, was appointed secretary of state at the Ministry of Public Service, replacing Stephen Yerima from Yambe. Three years later, Wango was retired from the civil service. He pleaded with Etende Zanga, the S.D.O., and Hansel Ebako, the Member of Parliament to intervene on his behalf so that he be given two more years of service. He was quite grateful when the Ministry of Public Service gave him two additional years beyond his retirement to go back to Government Bilingual High School Kumba, this time as an ordinary classroom teacher.

SIX

Général was hunched over the table, examining a number of documents. He always left the container door open whenever he was in. The single fluorescent bulb on the ceiling illuminated the interior of the container. He pushed the wheelchair away from the table and took out a book from the bookshelf behind him. He located some papers, adjusted the reading glasses on his face, and began making notes.

Outside, the night was quiet except for the chirp of crickets and the intermittent howl of a mongrel in the distance. A few minutes later the *Général* heard the distant rumble of the Douala-Yaoundé intercity train as it passed under one of the bridges somewhere in Olezoa. It was then that he heard the faint rustle of a man's footsteps on the grass outside. The footsteps approached nearer and stopped in front of the container. Then someone knocked timidly on the door.

"Yes," *Général* said, "come right in. You don't need to knock."

The pensioner stepped unsteadily into the container and sat down heavily on one of the chairs. He looked haggard. He didn't even look at *Général*. *Général* stopped what he was doing, removed his glasses, and put them on the table.

"What's the matter with you?" *Général* asked. "You don't look too well."

The pensioner sighed wearily. "I was at the ministry this morning and this afternoon too."

"Well, what happened?"

The pensioner looked up for the first time. He sent his hand into the raffia bag that was hanging on his shoulder and brought out a piece of paper. He stood up, walked across the container and handed the paper to *Général*. "Here, he said. The list of documents I need to put together for a new file. They gave it to me at Public Service."

Général put on his glasses again and unfolded the paper. He studied it briefly, removed his glasses, and looked at the pensioner. "You need these documents if they have to reactivate your file, calculate your arrears for these seven years, and begin paying your monthly pension."

"You don't understand," the pensioner said. "I don't have any of these documents with me. I left all of them in my hometown, and I'm four hundred and fifty kilometres from home. How would I have known my entire file would be missing in Public Service? They asked me to go to the broadcasting house and send an announcement home for the documents to be brought down to Yaoundé. Most people in my village go to farm very early in the morning and don't come home till late in the evening. And not everybody has a radio. Members of my family may not hear the radio announcement. A lot of things could happen. I'm finished. I tell you, I'm finished."

Général smiled. "Is that why you look so dejected?"

"You don't seem to regard what's happening to me with any seriousness at all," the pensioner said. His face was now creased in a frown. "That file is my life. I need my monthly pension and my arrears. The arrears in particular. I lived all my life in the city and never thought of retirement when I was in the civil service. I don't have a retirement home in the village. I began building a modest house a few years before I was retired. But I couldn't finish it. Its uncompleted walls stare at me disdainfully."

"I'm sorry," *Général* said. "I didn't mean to laugh at you. But you don't have to be so downcast. It doesn't help. If indeed your file is actually lost, there's nothing anybody can do about it. But they'll have vital records and other details about you in the ministerial archives. We could get them out of the archives in a couple of days, perhaps two or three. Give me some time to figure out what to do."

The pensioner began rubbing his hands. "Meanwhile, what do I do?"

"Just hang around. Pretend you're waiting for the real documents to be sent here by one of your relatives in the village."

"And how will you get my vital records from the archives? Why didn't they tell me this in the ministry?"

Général laughed again. "I've told you to leave it to me. There're a lot of things you don't know, hidden rules, a code of conduct that sustains the rusty machinery of the government. Outsiders like you don't fit in here. I've told you to leave things in my hands. Come back here in a week's time if the radio announcement to your village does not yield any results."

The pensioner stood up. *Général* adjusted his wheelchair and edged himself closer to the table. He picked up his glasses, put them on, and resumed reading. The pensioner stepped out of the container without another word.

Around 10:30 PM, a group of men began filing in slowly into the container. *Général* was still reading and making notes when they walked in. They sat down with the apologetic temperament of people who didn't want to disturb a busy man.

The first man wore a black beret and had a false diamond earring pinned on his left ear. He limped slightly on his left side.

The second man had a smooth face with puffy jaws and a double chin. A small tuft of hair was emerging from his chin. He wore a baggy jeans suit and a single, knitted, multicoloured driver's glove on his left hand. He had been smoking a cigarette when he approached the container. He threw away the unfinished cigarette just before he stepped into the container.

The third man had a thin narrow face. His artificial dreadlocks were partly hidden by a black face cap. He had a protruding jaw line and a scrubby moustache with a dishevelled beard. He held a black bag in his right hand.

The fourth man wore baggy gabardine trousers with a red, green, and yellow polythene windbreaker. He wore imitation stiletto-shaped crocodile skin boots and appeared to be suffering from an unknown ailment.

The fifth man was a tough-looking young man of about twenty-five. He wore a brown face cap that hid the upper part of his face and covered his eyes. His shirt sleeves were severed from the shoulders to expose bulging biceps and strong forearms. He too wore a pair of tattered jeans adorned with holes.

The sixth man wore a frayed grey suit. His face was covered with dark freckles. He held a black briefcase in his right hand.

They all sat quietly and waited. After ten minutes *Général* closed the book he had been reading and put it aside. He looked up at the men.

"You, Omnisports," *Général* said, calling the first man in the name of the city district he controlled. The man in the black beret stood up. "Report of the day."

The man in the beret crossed his hands behind his back as he spoke. "Two men were found dead in my area last night."

"How far apart? Do you know anything about their deaths?"

"No, *Général*. We have never seen them before. The police have not approached my boys. Their bodies were found about five kilometres apart."

"No connection," *Général* said. "They don't concern us."

The man sat down. *Général* looked round. "Biyem-Assi." The man with the crocodile boots stood up and put his hands behind his back. "What's happening in your zone?"

"We've had more robberies," the man said.

"What kind of robberies?"

"Twenty homes have been broken into, more than six cars stolen, mostly in the night, in the Sic housing estate."

"Any other thing?"

"The government has begun selling land at the outskirts of Mendong. I thought I should let you know."

"Yes, yes," *Général* said. He swung the wheelchair slightly to his left, opened a drawer, brought out a black diary and scribbled the information on it. He put the diary away and the man in the crocodile boots sat down.

"And you, Mokolo. What's happening in your sector?"

The man with the dreadlocks stood up and bowed solemnly. He picked up the black bag and emptied its content on the floor. *Général* craned his neck forward. Four passports, a gold necklace, jewellery, and an assortment of US dollars and Euro were littered on the floor.

"Let me see the passports and the money."

The man picked up the passports and the currency. He walked up to the table and handed them to *Général*. When he went back to his former position, he said, "Two thousand dollars and five thousand Euros. I didn't look at the passports."

Général looked at the passports. "American, German, Japanese, British," he said, as he flipped through the pages of one passport after another. He barely touched the foreign currency. When he looked up, there was a severe expression on his face.

"Mokolo!"

"*Général.*"

"Where did this foreign currency and passports come from?"

"I ..." the man hesitated. He fixed his gaze on the ceiling.

"Mokolo," *Général* said, "you're talking to me, not the ceiling. Did you hear me?"

The man began trembling. "*Général*, it's ... it's the new boys you asked me to recruit."

Général banged his fist on the table. "Shut up with your

recruitment nonsense! You had your orders. And orders are orders. No pick-pocketing around Mokolo. Those were your orders. And I warned all of you to leave foreigners alone. Mokolo market is a tourist centre. I restricted pick-pocketing to Mvog-Mbi and Poste Centrale. What do I do with these passports now? I've told all of you over and over. I don't want the police poking in their dirty noses in this place. And besides, robbing tourists gives a bad name to this country. You should have told your recruits."

"It was not until—" Mokolo tried to explain.

"Shut up and sit down," *Général* said. "Put the passports and money back in the bag and give it to me." Mokolo put the passports and money in the bag and gave it to him. *Général* placed the bag on the table and Mokolo sat down with his eyes fixed on the floor.

"And what about you?" *Général* asked, turning to the man with the double chin. "What's happening in Etoudi?"

The man stood up. "More car thefts, *Général*. Two of my boys have managed to infiltrate the gang. There's evidence that highly placed police officers and senior army officers are directing the operations. They're supplying gangs with guns and communication equipment. I'm still gathering more information."

"Guns in the hands of the wrong people in the city? Car thefts and unexplained deaths? And ten armed robberies in the short span of two weeks in broad daylight? I don't like it," the *Général* said. "This is not the Yaoundé I used to know. It's not good for business. I suspected the army and police were involved in this. Well, you're doing a good job. Keep it up. And what's happening in Mvog-Mbi?"

The tough-looking young man was on his feet even before Etoudi sat down. He had a no-nonsense air around him. He pushed his cap slightly with the index finger of his right hand to expose his eyes. He looked at *Général* straight in the face.

"There's a lot of trouble at Mvog-Mbi," he said, with the severity of someone delivering the news of a serious car accident

Général detected the severity in his voice. He pushed the wheelchair from behind the table and rolled it towards the men.

"Idris is out. He came out from Kondengui more than six months ago," the tough-looking lad explained. "He has managed to put together the remnants of his old gang."

"That's not good news," *Général* said. There was a frown on his face. "Why did it take you all this time to know Idris was out of prison?"

"He went underground as soon as they let him out," the lad went on. "He only surfaced when his gang was fully operational. In fact, they're gradually moving into our territory. His boys are already in Mvog-Mbi.

"What?" *Général* exclaimed.

"That's not all. He's moved into the zoua zoua market."

"I have a monopoly over the sale of *zoua zoua* in Yaoundé. He knows that."

"I went over to his place. Look, I told him, *Général* is the only one who distributes smuggled fuel from Nigeria here. He ordered me to leave before his boys threw me out."

"What's his price?"

"Three hundred and fifty-five francs."

"That's fifty francs below our distribution price! He's going to take over the market."

"We have to take action," the young man suggested. "But we have to lure him out of his headquarters."

"I want him brought here. You must do that as soon as you can. And what about your bike? Has it been repaired?"

"Not yet, *Général*. Yamaha has run out of original spare parts."

"Do everything to get the bike fixed. Check the Chinese and Belgian spare parts. Meanwhile, get in touch with your boys and devise a strategy. I want Idris brought here. You understand? Right here! And that's an order."

He turned the wheelchair round and rolled it back to its former position behind the table. "If there's nothing else, you can all go. I've taken note of your reports. I'll take whatever action is necessary."

The men did not move. "I say you can all go now." The man in crocodile skin boots shuffled his feet nervously. He stared at the floor. *Général* observed that something was amiss. The men did not want to leave. "What's the matter, Biyem-Assi? Look at me when I'm talking to you."

Biyem-Assi stood up.

"Yes, I'm listening. What's the matter?"

"I want to ... we ... we think we should have an increase in our monthly salaries."

"A salary increase?" *Général* looked surprised. "On top of the twenty-five thousand francs, I pay each of you every month?"

He looked at the faces of the other men. "Whose idea is it?" None of the men answered.

Général turned to the lad. "Mvog-Mbi?"

He stood up. "*Général.*"

"What do you know about this matter? Is this a conspiracy?"

A faint smile appeared on the young man's face. "It's not a conspiracy, *Général.*"

"Then what's it? I want to know."

"It was Biyem-Assi's idea, *Général.* He didn't know how to ask for more money from you."

"More money for what?"

The lad looked at Biyem-Assi. "Go on, tell him."

"Tell me what?" *Général* inquired. "Listen, I don't have time to fool around with you." His voice was edged with impatience. "I've got a lot of work to do."

"He put a girl in the family way," the young man said. "Daughter of a Colonel in the presidential guard."

"How many months?"

"Two, *Général.*" Biyem-Assi said. His face was ashen, his voice barely audible.

"And she wants an abortion, yes?" *Général* asked.

"Yes, *Général*."

"Well, you should have come out clean and told me, instead of the salary increase nonsense." He opened a drawer on the desk and brought out a wad of clean bank notes. He counted out fifty thousand francs and held the money out to Biyem-Assi. The man came forward, bowed, and took the money with both hands. *Général* picked up one of his business cards from the table. "Take the girl tomorrow to the Mfoundi clinic. Tell Dr. Essono I sent you. Give him my card."

Biyem-Assi took the card from *Général*. There was an expression of utter gratefulness on his face. "I don't know how to thank you, *Général*," he muttered.

"Don't thank me. Next time it will be AIDS you'll pick up," *Général* said sarcastically. "And when that happens don't come back here."

The men stood up and trooped out of the container. The man in the grey suit stayed behind. When the last man had left, *Général* asked him to pull his chair nearer.

"Well?" *Général* said finally.

"I collected rents from five tenants this week. The drainage pipes in the second house in Bastos, the one near the Swiss Embassy, need some minor repairs. I've already hired a plumber. He'll do the work this weekend. He flipped open his briefcase and brought out two bank deposit books. He handed them to *Général*. I deposited the money yesterday and today."

Général checked the books carefully before he put them away in a drawer. "Anything else?"

"Yes. There're rumours that the National Bank of Commerce may fold up. They're already having liquidity problems. I thought I should let you know."

"What options do I have?" *Général* asked him.

"You either leave the money in the Bank of Commerce or withdraw your deposits and open a new account in another bank."

"What do you recommend?"

"Withdraw the money," the accountant said. "I'm certain the bank will fold up."

Général remained silent for a while before he said, "How much do I have as savings in the Bank of Commerce?"

"Ten million, two hundred and fifty-five thousand francs."

"You sure the bank will fold up?"

"I'm quite certain," the accountant said.

"All right then, withdraw my savings tomorrow and deposit them in my other bank."

"I'll do so," the accountant said. "Oh, I almost forgot. Mr. Assuma, the director in the Ministry of Public Service has still not paid rents for the other house."

"The sixth month, isn't it?"

"Yes, sir. I've been to his office about three times this month."

"What date is it today?" *Général* asked.

"The twentieth."

"I'll give him about a week or so, and then I'll pay him a personal visit if that's what he wants," *Général* said. "That's all, I suppose."

"Yes, sir."

Général opened another drawer, brought out a cheque booklet and wrote the accountant a cheque. He signed it, tore out the leaflet, and handed it to him.

The man glanced at the cheque and looked at *Général*. "Oh, sir?" *Général* looked up. "You've added fifty thousand francs on top of my regular monthly salary."

"Yes," *Général* said. "A little incentive for your honest services and dedication to what you're doing for me. Good accountants are hard to come by these days."

"Thank you very much, sir." He stood up.

"Before you go, can you do me a favour? Go to Briqueterie and tell Bosco and Gaston to come here on the morning of the 28th. At 8 PM. I'll need their help to pull this wheelchair up the eighth floor of Public Service."

The accountant nodded. "I'll tell them. Six months of rents is a lot of money."

With that last word, the man picked up his briefcase and walked out of the container. *Général* adjusted himself on the wheelchair and settled down to do some work. When he looked at his watch, it was passed 10 PM. He took his cell phone and dialed a number. A few seconds later he said, "You can come and take me now." He gathered up the passports, the foreign currency, and the bag, and locked them away in one of the boxes behind him. He began tidying up the scattered sheets of paper on the table. He inserted a bookmarker on the page of the book he had been reading and put it back on the shelf. It was close to 10:15 PM when a man in a driver's uniform and cap walked quietly into the container. He removed the cap from his head before he sat down. *Général* glanced at his watch again. It was exactly 10:20 PM.

SEVEN

There is something fascinating, almost hypnotic about the city at nightfall. The long endless rows of electric poles and their overhanging street lights. The rush hour traffic that never ceases to amaze new comers to Yaoundé. Even at this hour, seven o'clock in the evening, it's a fluid bright stream of car taillights. Several cars behind each other, bumper to bumper. What a sight! An endless metallic serpent, stretching out of sight. And the flickering neon lights of the high-rises: CAMTEL, EMS, CASINO, SNI, IBM, CNR, BRICOLUX, CNPS, SGBC, HILTON, MAHIMA. They beckon alluringly, enticing the unwary to their vertiginous heights.

An unannounced fog descends gradually over the high-rises. The subdued street lights are now surrounded by shapely haloes, and the hazy neon lights on top of the high-rises flicker uncertainly. The blue, red, and amber twinkles are now eerie, fuzzy patterns against the foggy night sky. The ubiquitous taxicabs crawl along in uninterrupted yellow rows, their arrogant drivers swearing and cursing other drivers and pedestrians who block their way.

The pensioner wondered whether he should take a taxi. He had been warned several times that it was not safe at night, particularly for an old man like himself. Except for the long rows of frustrated, underpaid civil servants waiting to board the overcrowded municipal buses, and the monotonous snarl of the serpentine traffic, the city centre looked normal enough. The pensioner did not feel threatened. He looked at his watch. It was not yet 8 PM. He decided to walk. He crossed the street and stood in front of the SNI building. The cathedral and Casino Supermarket were behind him now. He walked towards the Mfoundi market and took a shortcut to the right, just before the market. He walked slowly, frequently glancing around him. It took him only fifteen minutes to go through the shortcut. Then he found himself at Mvog-Ada.

It was a new kind of life when the pensioner got to Mvog-Ada. The enticing smell of grilled fish, *bobolo*, *beignet*, *suya*, roasted plantains and coco yams assailed his nostrils. It was a tickling, inviting, and overpowering smell. Suddenly he felt very hungry. He walked over to a small group of women lined along the road and bought one grilled fish and one bundle of *bobolo*. He adjusted the raffia bag around his shoulder and began to peel off the leaves from the *bobolo*. He cut a portion of the *bobolo* and stuffed it into his mouth. Then he started tearing off small portions of the fish, spitting out the bones on the sidewalk as he chewed.

He had hardly eaten half of the fish when a group of six street children surrounded him. They came out of nowhere. One moment he was throwing away the *bobolo* leaves in a garbage container by the street. The next moment the children appeared out of the shadows of the night. Two of them tugged at his trousers. One held him by his shirt sleeve. Even in the faint street lighting, he noticed their emaciated looks. The oldest among them was barely 12-years old.

"One hundred francs, *Monsieur*. Give me something. I haven't eaten all day," one of them cried.

"Give me some fish. I have nothing to eat," another one begged.

He tried to shake them off, but they clung to him with determined tenacity. One of them commenced pulling his bag.

"Hey, leave my bag alone."

Another small boy who was clinging to him jumped up and hit his left hand. The cement paper in which the fish was wrapped jerked out of his hand and fell on the pavement. In an instant, like mongrel dogs, the whole lot of them fell on the dirty pavement and scrambled for the remains of the fish. One of them stood up triumphantly and brandished the now scattered remains and skeleton of the fish in the air. Then he ran across to the other side of the street. The others gave chase and pursued the victor. In a few minutes, they vanished in the shadowy tenements from which they had come.

It was so quick and sudden that the pensioner wondered whether it was a hallucination. His oily fingers and the *bobolo* were the only evidence that he had been eating something. He picked up the cement paper in which the fish had been wrapped and cleaned his fingers with its dry edges. Then he threw the remaining *bobolo* in the garbage dump. On second thought, he decided to have a beer to wash down the remnants of the fish and *bobolo* in his throat. He crossed the street and walked into the Eldorado. He ordered a beer and sipped it slowly as he looked at the night life around him. He ordered a second beer when the waiter came to take away the first bottle. It was getting close to 7:30 PM when he left the Eldorado. He crossed the street again and began walking unsteadily. He turned right at the junction and walked towards Nkolndongo, on his way to the long stretch of broken tarmac to Anguissa.

* * *

It was close to 8 PM when he got to the container. *Général* was alone when he walked in. He sat behind the table, sealing a document with a rubber stamp when the pensioner walked in.

"I thought you'd come before today," *Général* said.

"I've been trying to know the city. This evening I took a long walk to see what it looks like at night. My legs are tired, but it was refreshing." He sat down as he spoke.

"I see. It's not safe for an old man to walk around in the night, you know. Have you eaten anything?"

"Yes. Some fish." He wanted to talk about the children who had assaulted him and seized the fish. But he changed his mind. "You asked me to see you today," the pensioner added.

"Did I? Of course, I did." He turned the wheelchair round and reached for a large blue file on the shelf behind him. He put the file on the table and looked at the pensioner. "Guess what we have here."

"Don't tell me it's my file?"

Général chuckled. "It is."

"I don't want to believe it. How did you do it?" There was an incredulous look on the pensioner's face.

"My contact got it from the Public Service archives. She photocopied all the documents for me."

"How can I thank you?"

"It's not yet time to thank me," *Général* said. "You still have a long way to go. First of all, you have to make certified true copies of these documents." *Général* opened a drawer and brought out a thick manila folder. He uncovered it and began sorting out blank forms from the several papers in the folder. "How many children do you still have in school?" he asked the pensioner.

"Four. In secondary school."

"You'll need four certified true copies of their birth certificates." He gave the pensioner the first set of four blank forms. "You'll need these four forms to show that your children are still in school, and these other four to show that they are alive." He gave the pensioner two additional forms. "Here," he said, "one for a copy of your marriage certificate, and the other to show where you are domiciled." Finally, he gave the pensioner a blank sheet of paper. "You'll use this to write a fresh application for your pension."

"I'll need to buy stamps tomorrow," the pensioner said.

"Ah, yes. Fiscal stamps. How could I forget? You don't have to. I have a good supply here. A one thousand francs fiscal stamp for each form and one for the application."

The pensioner nodded.

Général opened another drawer and brought out a bunch of counterfeit fiscal stamps. He gave them to the pensioner and handed him the blue file and a bic ball point pen. "You can fill out all the blank forms and write the application right here. Turn around and use one of those chairs as a writing table."

The pensioner pulled one of the chairs, put down his bag on the floor, and opened the blue file. He first wrote out an application for his pension and then began filling out the forms from the information in the photocopied forms in the blue file. When he finally finished, he detached the fiscal stamps from the bunch *Général* gave him. He licked them and stuck them, one after the other, on the application and the rest of the forms. When he finished, he looked up.

"And don't forget to add your latest pay voucher to the file when they have all been certified," *Général* reminded him.

"I won't forget. I'll have to go to the *préfecture* to get all these copies certified tomorrow."

Général laughed. "Go to the *préfecture* by yourself? They won't certify them without the originals. And no one knows you there." He handed the pensioner an envelope. "While you were filling the forms I scribbled a note to the *préfet*. What day is it today?"

"Thursday."

"Go to the *préfecture* at Longkak first thing tomorrow morning. Make sure you give this to the *préfet*."

As the pensioner took the envelope, they heard the shuffle of several feet and voices outside. *Général*'s men entered the container one after the other, in a single file. They were only five of them tonight. The man in the brown suit was not among them.

The pensioner looked at the strange men. They sat down without uttering a word to him or *Général*. He wondered who they were. He thought it was time for him to leave. Perhaps they had come for some private spiritual consultations. He looked at his watch and stood up. It was almost 9 PM.

"As soon as the forms are certified, come back and see me on Saturday evening."

"Tomorrow is Friday. I don't want to lose a whole day. I could come here in the afternoon."

"This place is closed in the afternoon. My business here begins in the night, after seven. Fridays and Saturdays are too busy. Come back here on Monday or in the middle of the week."

The pensioner wanted to say something else, but he kept quiet. He thanked *Général* and left. It was quite dark when he stepped outside, but he knew the direction of the path that led back to the road. He sensed some presence in the bushes nearby, but it was too dark to see anything.

He walked until he came out on the main road near the *Rio bar d'Anguissa*. He walked slowly down the small dirt road that led to his nephew's house. As he walked down the road, he wondered how he could ever repay Kemcha and his family for accommodating and tolerating him for so long in their home. He didn't realize that Kemcha's overcrowded house, which was in the slums of Anguissa, was a two-room house until his fourth day in Yaoundé when he got up from his room at night to use the toilet. He missed his way and instead found himself in the living room. He was shocked to see Kemcha's wife and five children sleeping on three mats that were spread on the floor in the living room. Kemcha himself was asleep and snoring loudly on an old, sagging couch.

The next day when he got up in the morning, the children had all gone to school and Kemcha's wife had gone to the market. Kemcha had not yet gone to his provision store where he sold goods at Mokolo market.

When he entered the living room, Kemcha was there, watching a programme on TV. He greeted the pensioner in their native language. "Pa, you got up so late. I was waiting for you to wake up. How did you sleep?"

"I didn't sleep well at all," the old man said. "I was tired. Going up and down those stairs in the ministry exhausted me. Where's Eli?"

"She's gone to the market. The children have all gone to school. I was waiting for you to have your breakfast before I go to my store."

"That's very kind of you," the old man said. "Last night, I got up to use the toilet. But I missed my way and found myself in the living room. I didn't know that the children sleep on the floor, that you and Eli left the bedroom for me. You should have allowed me to sleep on the couch—"

"Pa—"

"No, listen. It's not proper to give up your bedroom and bed to me. I don't deserve it."

"Pa, we've not forgotten our culture and tradition, even here in the city. That's what I teach my children, to respect their elders. That's why they bring you water to wash your hands every evening before you eat."

"But with a big family like the one you have," the old man said, "life is not easy in Yaoundé."

"It's not easy, Pa. We're barely managing. But it's the spirit of giving and sharing that matters to us, particularly when we are blessed to host an elderly relative like you."

He thought of how much he would give Eli to buy food for the household and nice clothes for herself and the children when they pay his arrears. A hundred and fifty thousand francs? Two hundred and fifty thousand? How does one thank one's host who has deprived himself and his family of the little they have and given so freely? How does one say thank you to such a family?

He was so immersed in his thoughts that he didn't realize he had already arrived at Kemcha's house. It was Kemcha's neighbour's dog that brought his thoughts back to the present moment. The dog always barked when strangers passed by the road at night.

EIGHT

As soon as the pensioner left, Etoudi and the other men began giving their reports of the day. After they had finished, Mokolo said he had brought a client who wanted some personal consultation.

"What kind of client?" *Général* demanded.

"He's from the Presidency, *Général*. He approached me through several contacts. He says he needs your help very badly," Mokolo explained.

"Well, bring him in," *Général* said sternly. "I don't have time to waste."

Mokolo went out and came back shortly with a thin man. The man blinked his eyes several times before he sat down timidly on the chair Mokolo showed him.

"And what can I do for you?" *Général* asked in a flat voice.

"I ..." the man hesitated, "I need ... I need help."

"What's your name?" *Général* asked the man.

"Mvogo."

"Ah, *Monsieur* Mvogo. I hear you're from the Presidency."

"Yes," the man responded. "I have a niece who has been struggling to enter the Ecole Normale for the past three years. I want you to get her a place there."

"Ah, the Ecole Normale! Bambili, Yaoundé, or Maroua?" *Général* asked. A faint smile now hovered around the corners of his mouth.

"The higher *Ecole Normale* in Yaoundé."

"You know how much it will cost you, I'm sure. Most of the money will be used to procure the exam papers in the series she hopes to write. By the way, what series does she want to write?

"Geography," Mvogo said.

"No problem. My consultation fee is two million five-hundred thousands."

"I'm prepared to pay anything."

"And why do you want your niece to become a trained teacher? Is that what she wants to be?"

"What children want to be in life doesn't matter much these days. It's more than six years now that she's been sitting at home without a job, after her *Maîtrise*. Her father died when she was in secondary school. I raised her as my own child. She can't stay at home for the rest of her life. I'm told you have the right contacts."

"When will the entrance exam be launched?" *Général* asked nonchalantly.

"Soon," Mvogo said. "In a month or two."

"Let me know when she fills the application forms."

"I'll do that when the time comes. I'll do exactly as you say. I ..." the man hesitated, "I also have another case, a younger cousin. He needs the GCE certificate."

"That will cost you quite a lot. Much more than your niece. The certificates and results slips are much more difficult to fabricate. Ordinary or Advanced level?"

"Advanced level," Mvogo said. "Three papers. History, Literature and Economics. I want him to enter the university and read Law."

"It will cost you three and a half million. Has he written the exam before?"

"Several times. And he did not pass even one paper. He's a bright young man. We all know that. We've been everywhere, seen several native doctors. They all come up with the same thing. Someone in the family, on my father's side, does not want him to make any progress in life."

Général smiled wryly. "I'll need his national identity card, a copy of his birth certificate and a copy of his last results slip. Bring them to me as soon as you can."

"I brought an advance of two million francs for the two cases," Mvogo began. He reached for the breast pocket of his striped grey suit. "I can pay—"

"I only accept total payment after the job is completed," *Général* cut in. There was a tone of finality in his voice. He turned the wheelchair slightly and glanced at Mokolo.

"Okay," Mokolo said, nodding at Mvogo, "let's go. I'll take you back to your car on the road." The man stood up and followed Mokolo out of the container. After about ten minutes, Mokolo came back. The men hung around the container until close to ten thirty when the man in the chauffeur's uniform walked into the container. As soon as he came in, *Général* tidied up his table, rolled the wheelchair to the door of the container, and signalled Mokolo to put out the light. Two other men lifted *Général* and the wheelchair and placed it outside. Mokolo came out and latched the door of the container shut. The two men lifted the wheelchair again and carried it to the road. The chauffeur had already gone ahead of them. When they got to the road, a black Mercedes E280 was packed opposite the *Rio bar d'Anguissa*. The bar was still open, but the intersection was less busy. The chauffeur had already opened one of the back doors and the boot. Two of the men removed *Général* from the wheelchair, tucked him in the car's open backseat and closed the door. The chauffeur folded the wheelchair and placed it in the boot. He closed the boot and entered the car. Three of the men crossed the street and entered the bar. Mokolo opened the front door of the Mercedes and sat next to the chauffeur. Etoudi went in behind and sat with *Général*, keeping a comfortable distance between *Général* and himself.

"All right," *Général* said, "let's go."

The chauffeur turned on the ignition and started the car. "Where to, *Général?*" he asked, speaking for the first time.

"To Obili," *Général* said. There was a distant look in his face. The chauffeur eased the car into the road and drove away into the night.

It was getting to midnight when the Mercedes arrived Obili. The car crept past *Palais de Verre* and came up to Obili. The day at Obili was just beginning. The place was alive with revellers. The night buses travelling to Bamenda were getting ready to depart. Music from several bars was blaring in the night, and the night taxis were busy dropping passengers at the T-junction. It seemed everyone was converging at Obili. The approach of midnight appeared to be the signal for the interminable flow of human traffic. The fish, pork, and chicken customers; the *suya*, kolanut, bitter kola, and cigarette vendors; the hookers, the scammers in the cyber cafés, and the money doublers were now wide awake as the rest of the city slept.

The chauffeur drove past a bus stop and turned left. He tried as much as possible to avoid parking next to a garbage container as he eased the car to a stop at the edge of the tarmac, in the direction to Chapelle Obili. He switched off the ignition. The three men sat still in the car and waited. After five minutes the chauffeur began tapping his fingers nervously on the steering wheel. Another five minutes went by. Mist began accumulating on the car's cold windscreen.

Mokolo coughed once to clear his throat. He turned and looked at *Général*. "*Général*, I think someone should call the woman. She should have known by now that you're here."

"You called to let her know I was coming, didn't you?"

"Yes, *Général*, I did. But she's ten minutes late."

"Give her another ten minutes. The night looks very busy She must have a lot of clients on a night like this. She'll come."

They waited again for another ten minutes. Etoudi was the

first to notice the dark silhouette of a short stocky woman detach itself from a distant alleyway. He pointed out the woman through the mist-covered car screen. *Général* gave the chauffeur an order to lower his window. The chauffeur turned on the key and pressed a button. The right window of the car slid down gradually.

"That's enough," *Général* said. The glass was almost all the way down. The woman walked deliberately towards the Mercedes, her large hips undulating from side to side in a calculated motion. She came up to the car and walked round to the other side. Then she leaned forward and stuck her face in the car.

"*Bonsoir, mon beau*," she said. "I'm so sorry to have kept you waiting. It's a very busy night as you can see."

"*Bonsoir*, Claire." *Général* wriggled his nose as the strong cigarette odour from her mouth invaded the rich leather interior of the Mercedes. "How's the market tonight?"

"Quite rich and plentiful, I can say. Lots of variety. But prices have gone up a bit."

"Again?" *Général* was surprised.

"We now have an AIDS-free warranty, that's why. Life has no spare parts, you know. Tough shots like you should not complain. Prices have gone up everywhere. We must struggle to survive."

"How much have you added?"

"Only twenty-five thousand francs."

"Twenty-five thousand! Well, but I want something different. A little bit juicy."

"Why?" There was a look of surprise on the woman's face. "Henriette has always been reserved for you. No other man touches her. You seem to have forgotten her."

"Henriette has long fingers. I didn't intend to tell you. But you had to know eventually. Took money from my pockets the other time, while I was dozing. I only found out after my chauffeur had taken her away."

"The little devil!" the woman cursed softly. "She did that?

Despite the handsome commission that I pay all of them? Stealing from my *patron*? She'll have to answer for that one."

"It's nothing. It was close to Christmas time. I'm sure she needed the extra money. A little incident I've forgotten. But I need a change tonight. A young body. My senses are dulled. I want some stimulation for my mind. I'm prepared to pay an extra bonus."

"Let me think," the woman said. "You mind if I smoke?"

"Not with your head in the car," *Général* retorted.

The woman laughed. She pulled out her head and brought out a packet of cigarettes and a lighter from her pocket. She pulled out a cigarette and lit it. Then she inhaled deeply and blew out smoke rings into the night sky, her head cocked at a conceited, defiant angle. She continued smoking for a while, the fingers of her left hand beating an irregular beat on the car's roof. After a while, she tapped off a long piece of cigarette ash on the ground before she thrust her head back into the car.

"What time is it?" she asked.

"Close to twelve-thirty," Mokolo replied.

"Can you give me twenty minutes? Will you be patient enough to wait? I'll surprise you. Your senses will meet their wildest dreams tonight."

There was a look of excitement on *Général*'s face. "I'll wait," he said, "I'll wait."

The woman pulled her face out of the car and strode away purposefully. She went back the same way she had come and faded away in the darkness. *Général* leaned his head back on the car's seat, closed his eyes and relaxed.

He drifted off to sleep. Etoudi shook him three times before he opened his eyes. "*Général*," he said, "they're here. Claire is back."

His eyes barely had enough time to focus as Claire came up to the car with a slim, fair complexioned, pretty girl of about twenty-two. He just had time to notice the smooth legs the girl's short leather mini skirt exposed and her cone-shaped arrogant

116

breasts that clamoured for attention against her tight, white cotton blouse. An imitation gold crucifix hung down from a chain around her small neck. The crucifix dangled in the small valley where her two breasts rose from her chest. Claire blocked his view when she thrust her head into the car.

Général managed to catch his breath. "Who's she?" he asked as he rubbed his eyes.

There was a crafty smile on Claire's face. "I had to go very far for her. They're hard to get. She comes with a price. You must be prepared to pay—"

"Anything. I'll pay anything. Who's she?"

"Marie-Noel. Second year university student. It took a lot of persuasion. I had to offer her an advance. She's very expensive. AIDS-free guarantee too. This is her first time in the market. And she's for you alone."

"You're standing in my way. Let me see her."

Claire removed her head from the car and said, "Come on, my darling, the boss wants to see your charming figure."

The girl swayed her full hips provocatively as she walked up to the car. She leaned forward and blew *Général* a kiss. The sharp smell of the perfume she wore pervaded the interior of the car. Mokolo and the chauffeur shifted uncomfortably in their seats. The *Général* raised his right hand and slowly caressed her cheek and nose with his fingers. Then he brushed her small lips with his thumb. The girl's lips twitched momentarily and *Général* let out an ecstatic sigh.

"Let her come inside."

Etoudi opened his own side of the door and came out. He held the door open. The girl took her time getting into the car. She pushed in her hips in the car first, and then pulled in her thighs and feet after her. Etoudi could not help staring at her long smooth legs. He came in after her and closed the door. She looked at *Général's* round face and smiled. She fondled his smooth jaw

with her right hand and kissed him lightly on his lips. *Général*
sighed again and turned to Claire. He brought out a wad of notes
and gave it to her.

She didn't even count the money before she put it away. "How
much?" she asked.

"One hundred."

An expansive smile spread across her face. The chauffeur had
already started the car. It was purring slowly. Claire leaned down
again and brought her mouth close to *Général*'s ear. "Be very gentle
with her and treat her well," she whispered. "She'll provide your
senses with the proper stimulation, I promise you."

As she pulled out her head, the car's window began sliding
up. The car made a U-turn as its headlights came on. It made a
slow turn to the right and joined the advancing line of night traffic as it moved inevitably towards Melen, into the anonymity of
the waiting city.

It was close to 2 AM in the morning when the Mercedes
brought Marie-Noel back to Obili. The place was not as busy
as it had been at midnight. The long lines of yellow taxicabs had
reduced to a trickle. The girl planted a warm kiss on *Général*'s
right cheek before she came out of the car and closed the door. She
turned round and waved just as the Mercedes was pulling away.
She gripped her handbag closer to her body and looked around
her. There was a self-assured, satisfied smile on her face. Not even
Claire could guess that she had two hundred thousand francs in
her handbag. What a generous man. And it had been that quick
and easy. She would now be able to pay her rents for six months.
She would be able to buy the few additional things she needed
for her comfort. And of course, she still had the remaining part
of her commission to pick up from Claire. Thirty-five thousand
francs after deductions from the advance she had demanded.

She took quick easy strides as she began heading towards
Chapelle Obili. She thought of walking towards the lake, to take

the short cut that would take her to the university campus. She looked at her watch. On second thought, she walked back to the main road and raised up her hand, flagging down a motorbike to take her to the university residence.

* * *

Around 2:15 AM the Mercedes arrived Bastos. The car drove past the Russian embassy and turned left. It went down a small hill, crossed a makeshift bridge and came up to a small hill that had been levelled by a bulldozer. A narrow dirt road, covered with broken stones, ran opposite the hill. The Mercedes drove up the road and turned left on a driveway that entered the premises of a small picturesque house with a rich luxurious garden. Apart from the lights in the balcony, the rest of the house was dark. *Général* asked the chauffeur to hide the car from the front entrance so that it couldn't be seen by anybody coming up the driveway. The chauffeur turned the car slowly and parked it behind a small rose bush. The three men sat quietly and waited.

NINE

He was shopping at Casino with Mvog-Mbi pushing his wheelchair when he saw her for the first time. They were coming up the cosmetics aisle and she was coming down. Her looks and elegance were too striking for him to let her go without talking to her. He turned his head and said to Mvog-Mbi. "Leave me alone right now and follow me from a distance. I want to talk to that woman coming down the aisle." Mvog-Mbi stopped pushing the wheelchair and left.

When the woman was just a short distance from him, he raised his hand, waved it, and smiled. The woman smiled back. He pushed the wheelchair towards her and said, "Excuse me, but you look familiar, we must have met somewhere."

"Quite likely," the woman said. Her voice was smooth and sensuous and she had a generous smile on her face. She was as graceful as a gazelle, brown and slim, with elongated hands that tapered off into long slender fingers.

"You live here in Yaoundé?" *Général* asked her.

"Yes," she said, "in Mokolo." To his utter surprise, she said, "Can I help push the wheelchair? Which part of the supermarket do you want to go?" She went behind him, took hold of the wheelchair and spun it round. *Général* felt dizzy. This was a totally new experience. "Do you want to buy anything in particular?"

"Yes, yes," he said. "Cornflakes, wine, whole cream milk, sugar, bread—"

"Quite a lot of things," the woman said. "Who cooks for you?"

"I have a cook," he said, "but I like doing my own shopping."

"And your wife, what does she do?"

"I'm not married." Before she could continue, *Général* said quickly, "I don't have a woman in my life. I'm still looking for one."

"Oh!" she exclaimed.

They moved from one section of the supermarket to the other, looking for what he wanted to buy. She helped him take the items off the shelves. She stopped and moved in front of him. "You'll need a shopping trolley. Looks like you're buying a lot of things. I'll go get one."

When she left, *Général* beckoned Mvog-Mbi who was following from a discrete distance. Mvog-Mbi approached and said, "Yes, *Général*."

"Things are becoming a little bit complicated. I'm buying more things than I expected. She can't push the wheelchair and the trolley at the same time. Keep some distance behind me. I'll have to introduce you. Be courteous and respectful. Ah, there she comes with the trolley …"

The woman walked up to *Général* and said, "Here we are." She started pushing the trolley and suddenly she realized how awkward the situation was. "But …" she said, "I can't push the trolley and the wheelchair at the same time."

"I came with a young man who always assists me with the shopping. He's not far away from here. He must be nearby. As *Général* spoke, Mvog-Mbi came forward, stood in front of the woman and bowed graciously. "Good afternoon, Madam."

"Are you the one helping with the shopping?"

"I am, Madam."

"Okay, you push the trolley and I'll push chair."

"As you say, Madam." Mvog-Mbi glanced at *Général*. There was a contented smile on his face. He winked at Mvog-Mbi.

They were almost done with the shopping when *Général* suddenly remembered that he needed to buy a bottle of *Amarula*. He reminded Mvog-Mbi to get a bottle from the wine and liquor section. When they'd finished shopping and he'd paid for the items, she said "Where do I leave you? Will you take a taxi outside?"

"My car is in the parking lot. You didn't buy anything," he observed, as she continued pushing the wheelchair. Mvog-Mbi followed behind, pushing the overloaded shopping trolley.

"No," she said. "I was just window shopping. I come here to window shop when I don't have money to buy things."

When they got to the parking lot he said, "Can I drop you at Mokolo, where you live?"

"Yes, I'll appreciate it. Is this your car, this beautiful Mercedes?"

Général smiled. "It is."

Mvog-Mbi opened the boot and put the grocery bags in it. He opened the left back side of the car and asked the woman to get in. She went in and was surprised to see a uniformed chauffeur sitting behind the steering wheel. Mvog-Mbi closed the door and went to the other side. He helped *Général* into the backseat. He closed the door, put the wheelchair in the boot, went to the front seat, and sat with the chauffeur.

"Where to, *Général?*" the chauffeur asked.

"We'll go to Mokolo first and drop this lady. Where in Mokolo, my dear?" he asked her.

"Mokolo Elobi."

"To Mokolo Elobi," he repeated to the chauffeur. "Pass through Briqueterie. It will be shorter. There's too much traffic at Mokolo market."

"As you say, *Général*," the chauffeur said. He started the car and pulled out of the parking lot.

As the car drove down the 20th May Avenue, *Général* edged closer to the woman. "You haven't told me your name," he whispered in her ear. "You're a very beautiful woman, do you know that?"

She giggled and said, "Martina. My name is Martina."

"Is that your real name, *Général*?"

He hesitated momentarily before he said, "No, it's my city name."

"Your city name? What does that mean?"

He evaded her question and instead said, "What part of the country do you come from? Your English is so good."

"From Bafia. My father is Bafia; my mother was born in Bokito. But I grew up in Kumba, Ekona, Nyasoso, and other Anglophone towns, where my father was a *sous-préfet*, an Assistant District Officer, for several years."

"I see."

"And you?"

"I've lived in Yaoundé most of my life."

"But you're not Ewondo, Bulu or Eton, are you?"

"No, I'm not. I came from Menamo, a long time ago. We'll talk about it some other time."

The car was now at Mokolo Elobi. "Over there," she said. "You can drop me near the *pharmacie*." The chauffeur pulled the car gently to the sidewalk. Before she stepped out of the car, *Général* asked her for her cell phone number

"She gave him her phone number. Don't forget to call me," she said.

"I'll call you over the weekend," *Général* said as he entered the numbers into his cell phone. The chauffeur drove slowly up the road to Niki Mokolo before he turned right at the traffic lights on the road to Cité Verte and Madagascar.

*   *   *

It took about a month before they started seeing each other She came over to his house at Cité Verte for the first time over a weekend in May. He remembered vividly how they made love that evening. Her undulating hips, the tenderness of her caressing fingers, and the ecstasy in her voice when she was about to come pushed him into heights of rapturous pleasure that increased in tempo until he exploded inside her. Then he lost consciousness momentarily, not knowing where he was as he descended into a deep slumber. When he got up, she looked into his eyes with a half-smile and asked him to drink his favourite liquor—*Amarula*—which she had brought on a tray with ice cubes and a dash of cinnamon.

One Saturday night, at about 8 PM, he paid her a surprise visit at her place in Mokolo Elobi. Mvog-Mbi pushed the wheelchair through the mud on the small narrow pathway that went down to a small mud brick house in the miserable Elobi neighbourhood in which she lived—a neighbourhood that was always swamped with muddy water and sewage anytime it rained. Mvog-Mbi knocked on the thin plywood door.

"Who's it?" she asked.

"Open, it's me," Mvog-Mbi said.

She recognised Mvog-Mbi's voice and began opening the door. *Général* asked Mvog-Mbi to go back to the car. "Oh my God!" she said when she opened the door and saw who it was. "What brings you here? How did you find this place?" She tied a wrapper over her breasts which exposed her chest, shoulders and back. She reluctantly took the wheelchair and pushed it into the room. "I didn't want you to know where I live."

He was shocked when he entered the room. A single 13-Watt low energy Chinese-made bulb dimly illuminated the small room. A small wooden bed was set against one wall. There was only one chair in the room. Her assorted clothes hung on nails on another wall. A kerosene stove, a bunch of plantains, coco yams, tomatoes, a bottle of palm oil, cassava, and a variety of odd tins were scattered on the floor at the far end of the room, opposite the bed.

He wanted to say, 'you live in this rat hole?' instead, he said "Is this where you live? What do you do with all the mud and rain now that it's the rainy season? What do you eat? How do you survive? You said your father was an S.D.O, didn't you?"

She felt humiliated. She bowed down her head in shame. When she raised her head, she looked dignified and unapologetic.

"I didn't tell you I have a first degree, did I?" In political science from the university at Soa. My father retired from the civil service eight years ago. He built a comfortable retirement house in Bafia. I didn't believe it when my mother called me one evening and told me my father had married a second wife, a girl from neighbouring Ombessa. During the Christmas holidays, I went to Bafia to see things for myself. My father's second wife was just about my age. I tried to convince my mother to beat the shit out of her and throw her out of her matrimonial home. She said it will upset my father.

"Then leave him, for God's sake. How can you share the same man in the same house with a girl who is just barely my age?" I argued.

"You don't understand, Martina. I still love your father. I've stayed in this marriage for too long to quit because your father has a younger second wife." She countered

"Nothing I said would convince her. That's when I made up my mind to abandon them—my father and mother—and struggle to survive alone in Yaoundé. At twenty-eight, four years after I graduated with a degree from the university, this is where I find myself."

She bowed her head again as tears rolled down her cheeks. She wiped her face with the wrapper and looked up. "Well," she said, "at least say something."

Général looked subdued. "I'm sorry, he said, "I'm really sorry. I didn't mean to ... I didn't know—"

"That's okay." She had regained some of her composure.

"I'll like to leave now," he said. He brought out his cell phone and called Mvog-Mbi to come and take him.

Soon after, they had their first fight. She'd told him she didn't like condoms and that he should stop using them with her. They were in the living room in his house in Cité Verte, watching TV when Martina began the discussion.

"Why do you use condoms with me?" she asked. "What are you afraid of?"

He looked in her direction briefly and continued watching the evening news.

She took the remote control and switched off the TV. "You should listen to me when I'm saying something important."

He kept his calm. "Important?" he asked. "What's important in condoms?"

"You belittle everything I say, don't you?"

"No, no, don't get me wrong. On the contrary, I appreciate everything you say. It's important that I do. Could you put on the TV? I was watching the news. I want to know what's going on in the country."

"You haven't answered my question."

"Which was?"

"Why do you use condoms with me?"

"Because since we started seeing each other, we don't know our HIV status."

"Is that all?"

"Yes." He didn't want to tell her that he didn't want her pregnant, that he was afraid to have children with a woman.

"Why didn't you tell me all this time?"

"Well, I'm telling you now. As a matter of fact, I'd like you to do an HIV test. I'll send you to my doctor at the Mfoundi clinic tomorrow. I also want you to test for Chlamydia, Syphilis, and Hepatitis B."

"You think I have AIDS or am infected with STDs, don't you""

"Look, Martina, I simply want us to know our status. Let me show you my lab results."

"I don't have to see them. I'll go do the tests tomorrow." She switched on the TV and the news continued.

"Thank you," he said. "When you get to the clinic in the morning, go straight to Dr. Essono's office and tell him I sent you. He'll give you preferential treatment at the lab."

She came back two days later, on Friday night and showed him the results. She removed two envelopes from her bag and gave them to him. The first envelope contained the HIV result. It was negative. The results of the other three tests were negative.

"This should satisfy you now, I'm sure"

He held out his hand and asked her to come closer to him. He kissed her gently on her lips. "You still look unhappy," he said. "I hope you're not annoyed with me. It's not about satisfying me. It's about us. It's about mutual trust and confidence."

He rolled the wheelchair into his study and came back shortly with his own results from the lab. He gave her the two sheets of paper. "Here are my own results from Dr Essono's lab.

She took the papers and looked at the date on the results. They were just three weeks old. She put the papers on the table, lifted him from the wheelchair, and placed him on the upholstered chair opposite the TV. He was surprised at her strength.

"Is that how strong you are?" he asked her. "I weigh seventy-five kilograms. And you lifted me up so easily."

"My Bafia blood," she said. "Strength I inherited from my father's side. Where's Fouda? Is he in the kitchen?"

"No. He left when you called. I told him you were coming tonight."

"Fine," she said. "Call and tell him to take the weekend off."

"Why?" he asked.

"I'm going to spend the weekend here." Her face expanded into an affectionate sensuous smile. "I'll cook you some delicious

Bafia food and give you a good body massage."

Later on, after they ate supper, he called his men and told them he had cancelled consultations and daily reports at the container for the weekend. He also called Fouda, his cook, and told him he was travelling to Douala so he could take the weekend off.

The following week, he asked his accountant to contact housing agents to get him a comfortable three bedroom house in Bastos with two toilets, one bathroom, a kitchen, and a spacious balcony. The accountant located the house in a week. He got his men to equip the house in less than four days. He went there himself to inspect the furniture, curtains, kitchen equipment, beds and sheets. Everything was in place. The workers in the small garden in front of the house had finished the landscaping. They said the flowers will be in the garden the next day in the morning. On Saturday evening, the workers in the garden finished planting the grass and flowers.

He called Martina at two o'clock in the afternoon on Sunday. He knew she had come back from church and would be in the house.

"Yes?" she said when her cell phone rang. Almost immediately, she recognised his voice. "Oh, *Général*, darling. Where are you?"

"My car is on its way to your place. Something urgent has come up. I need to see you at once."

She was concerned with the tone of his voice. "Are you alright darling? Your voice sounds strange."

"I'm all right," he said. "You'll see the Mercedes in front of the *pharmacie*. Come up to the car and get into the back seat."

"What's it all about?" she asked.

"Just do as I say. I'll let you know the details later."

She walked up from her room to the Mercedes that was parked in front of *Pharmacie Elobi*. She entered and sat on the back seat and closed the door.

As soon as she got into the car, a man placed a black hood

over her head and held her mouth. "Please don't shout," the voice of the man said. "We're taking you somewhere. Don't panic. This is *Général*'s Mercedes. He's not in the car. You'll get the explanation later."

She didn't recognize the man's voice. She relaxed and the man relaxed his hold on her mouth and neck. The car drove around for about 20 minutes before it came to a stop. Two men brought her out of the car and walked with her for a short distance on a gravel driveway. Then they took her up a flight of stairs and opened a door. She felt she was in some kind of house. The door was closed behind her and the man who had spoken in the Mercedes removed the hood from her head. *Général* was in his wheelchair in a beautifully decorated living room adorned with satin curtains. He signalled the two men to go back to the car. The men went outside and left him alone in the house with Martina.

"What's going on darling?"

"It's a surprise," he said. "Go round and see the kitchen, bathroom, toilets and the bedrooms.

She did as he said, going from one room to the other. When she finished she came back to the living room and said, "don't tell me you've bought another house."

"I haven't," he said. "It's not my house. It's yours."

"Mine? Is this some kind of joke, *Général*?"

"It's not a joke, Martina. It's your house. You'll leave Mokolo Elobi and move here tomorrow."

"Tomorrow? This … this is—" She suddenly felt exhausted and sat down on one of the chairs in the living room.

Général became worried. "Are you okay Martina?"

"I'm fine," she said. "It's just that I… I never expected this. It's come as a shock."

"I'm sorry," *Général* said. "I should have told you. But I really wanted it to be a surprise."

She went down on one knee, hugged him tightly, and embraced

him. "Thank you, thank you so much. You don't know what you've done to me. You've transformed my life."

"Here," he said. "These are the keys to your house."

Later that evening, as the Mercedes dropped her off at Mokolo Elobi, she knew that in the next 24 hours, her life will be transformed for good.

* * *

Kevin was born on November 22nd at the Central Hospital at 3 AM. She tried to hold on to the contractions till morning, but couldn't as the interval between the contractions became shorter with every passing hour. She finally called him at 2:30 AM.

"Send the chauffeur to come immediately and take me to the hospital. I think the baby is on its way."

"I'll send him right away. He'll be there in ten minutes." Martina tried to hear what he was saying. Something seemed to be wrong with his voice.

She had prepared everything for the delivery—a baby's cot with a mosquito net in the house; disposable diapers, feeding bottles, a sterilizing unit, sheets, a blanket, woollen socks and caps, baby powder, gripe water. She made a mental review of each item as she put it in the baby's box before the chauffeur came. It was later on, when Dr Achu, her gynaecologist, had delivered the baby that she realised she had come to the maternity wearing only the dress she had on when the contractions began. She had no tooth brush or tooth paste, bathing soap, rubbing oil, comb, nightgown or towel. She had even forgotten her toilet bag. She arrived the hospital wearing only a pair of brown slippers.

Général only came to see the baby in her house in Bastos a week after she was discharged from the hospital. Initially, she thought he was quite busy with his business engagements in the city. On the night he came to her house, the baby was sleeping. He looked ill-at-ease when Martina wanted to go and bring the baby.

"No, no, don't," he pleaded. "You said he was asleep. I don't want to wake him up."

"He'll not wake up. He only gets up when it's his feeding time," Martina said. "You haven't even seen him, *Général*. Oh, he's so cute and really resembles you."

Général became more distressed. "I … I think I'll go. I'll see him some other time. I'm sorry, I have to leave now."

Martina knew something was terribly wrong when he kept away from seeing the baby for more than one month. She tried to figure out what it was, but couldn't. She called him persistently, pleading with him to come and see the baby. He only sent the accountant to give her money for her weekly supplies.

She waited until the baby was six months before she decided to confront him. That Sunday night, she went to his house at Cité Verte when she knew he would be watching the evening news. He had forgotten that she had a duplicate key to his front door so he was surprised when the front door opened suddenly and she burst into the living room with the baby who was fast asleep on her back.

"Here's your son. Take him!" she shouted as she unloosened the baby from her back and dumped him on a chair. The baby was fast asleep despite her shouting. "I say take him."

He was taken aback. Shocked. There was a harsh expression on his face. "What's this, Martina? What are you trying to do? Don't force me into anything. I won't touch him."

"You think I went out with another man and deceived you that I was pregnant?"

"I know the baby is mine."

"Then why don't you want him? Are you seeing another woman? That's it, isn't it? You're going out with another woman."

"Shut up, Martina. You know there's no other woman. Stop talking nonsense."

"You call your own son nonsense?"

"Take the child away! I don't want to see him!"

"If you don't want to see the child, what about me, what about us. At least, name the child. You're his father. Give me a name I'll use for his baptism."

"I can't think of a name now. Name him yourself. Listen, Martina, the birth of this child has only complicated my life. For heaven's sake, you're pushing me against the wall. Don't push me beyond what I can endure, otherwise, I'll explode."

She sat down wearily on the chair next to the baby and began to cry. She felt the tears burn her face as they rolled down her cheeks. After a while, she stood up, took the baby and strapped him back on her back. *Général*'s face was immobile, his mind impenetrable. She saw the uneasiness on his face and noticed how detached he was from the baby. Something was wrong, she thought, terribly wrong. This was not the *Général* she knew and loved before she became pregnant. She left the living room, walked out through the front door, and banged the door. As soon as she got outside, she hailed a taxi to take her back to her house in Bastos. It was in the taxi that she made up her mind not to care any longer about him. She'll leave him to exorcise whatever demons had taken over him. From now on, he'd have to sort out his own mess alone.

TEN

The engine of an approaching car disturbed the quietness of the morning. The car's tyres scrunched the gravel on the driveway as it came up the road. The car inched its way to the front of the house. The right front door swung open and the car's interior light came on. A woman kissed the driver in the car and came out. She closed the car door and walked up the front steps of the house. She took out a single key from her handbag and opened the front door. She turned round and waved at the man in the car before she entered the house. The car turned round slowly and drove away.

Général looked at his watch. "Okay," he said. "Take me there now." The chauffeur and the other two men came out of the Mercedes. The chauffeur opened the boot, brought out the wheelchair and unfolded it. Then Mokolo and Etoudi placed *Général* in the wheelchair and carried it up the stairs to the front entrance of the house. *Général* folded his hand into a fist and banged on the door with his knuckles, deliberately avoiding the visible door bell.

"Who is it?" Martina asked from inside the house.

He sensed the fear in her voice. "It's me. Come on, Martina, open the door!"

"What do you want?"

"Open the door," *Général* demanded again. "Don't keep me waiting outside."

A key turned in the lock and the door opened half-way. The head of the woman who had entered the house peeped outside.

"Well," she said, "it's you."

"Now that you know it's me, be decent enough and open the door." Martina opened the door wider. *Général* turned to the two men. "Leave me alone for a while and wait for me in the car." She closed the door as *Général* wheeled the chair into the house. *Général* looked around the spacious sitting room. It had a set of dark-brown upholstered leather chairs, one set of cane chairs, and was decorated with potted plants. White satin curtains were pulled across the spacious windows.

"Why do you keep doing this to me?" she burst out. "Always waiting for me in the shadows, finding out where I go, sending your men to follow me all over the town. I tell you, I'm sick of it all. You're a sick man, you understand. Why can't you leave me alone?"

"Will you shut up, Martina," *Général* said. "And stop yelling at the top of your voice. I don't want my men outside to hear all this."

"Why?" she asked. "Your double standards, as usual, enh?"

"I didn't come here to talk about double standards and my life," *Général* retorted. "Who was that man in the car? And while you're thinking of what lie to tell me? Let me have something to drink."

"There's no *Amarula* in the house."

"Well, can I have cold water? I'm thirsty."

Martina turned her face away and walked towards the dinning table. "There's no cold water. Is that why you're here, at four in the morning?"

"I can't even have a drink of cold water in *my* house?"

"*Your* house?" Martina said sarcastically. "Because you pay the rents for this damned place? If I had my way, I'll…"

"You'll do what?"

She did not answer. *Général* propelled the chair towards the kitchen door. He opened the door, went into the kitchen, and opened the fridge. He took out a bottle of mineral water and looked for a glass. He came back to the living room with the bottle and glass. He poured himself a glassful and drank the water. He placed the bottle and glass on the dinning table and propelled the wheelchair towards the upholstered chairs.

"Come over here and sit down. I've always told you not to talk to me when you're standing up like that. Come and sit down here."

Martina turned and walked back reluctantly. She sat down on a low chair opposite him. Their heads were now on the same level. He looked into her eyes.

"What is it you want? Why can't you leave me alone? Live your life the way you want it, and let me live mine my own way."

"Where is Kevin?" he asked.

"He's asleep."

"You leave a four-year old child alone in the house to go out and sleep with men in the city?"

The woman looked at him steadily in the face. Her eyes were defiant. "Perhaps if you lived in this house as his father, I'll not go out and sleep with men in the city. Don't you find it strange that your own child doesn't know you, doesn't know what you look like? How do I explain to him the existence of a father who only sneaks in here past midnight and disappears before dawn? All these years. How do you explain this kind of strange lifestyle to a child?"

He avoided the penetrating look of her big eyes. He turned the wheelchair round and went towards the table. He poured himself another glass of water. After he drank the water, he began turning the empty glass round and round with his hands.

"I didn't want children, you know that. I told you over and over. You trapped me into this. It was a trap, and I won't forgive you for it. It was your doing. Is this the father you want Kevin to know? These ... these shrivelled legs? Is this any kind of life? I am providing for him. That's sufficient."

"Why don't you give him a chance to know you? He'll come to accept you as you are and grow up to love you like I did—"

"Enough of that," *Général* cut in sharply. "I don't want to hear about your love rubbish. You know why you've always slept with me. It's the money, this house, what I provide to make your life comfortable."

"You know that's not true."

"I know a lot of things that are true." He banged the glass on the table and pushed the wheelchair towards her. "If other men want to enjoy the warmth and comfort that your tender flesh provides them, let them take care of you. This flirting has to stop." He gripped her wrist and shook it roughly. "You understand, it's got to stop!"

"Let go of my hand. You're hurting me."

"I could kill you for this. I could kill you. You know that." He released the tight grip on her wrist.

Martina began nursing her bruised wrist. "What use will I be to you if you kill me? What will happen to Kevin?"

"When you look at me, tell me, what do you see? A disabled man who sleeps with you, with whom you exchange sex for money? The father of your child? What do you see?"

"I see a man who is afraid to look in the mirror and see his own face. A man who is scared to confront himself. A man who's not a man."

Général slapped her hard across the face. "I've seen my face a thousand times in the treachery and viciousness of this city. I don't need you to remind me of what I look like."

She broke down and began to cry. Almost immediately *Général* regretted slapping her. He wanted to go and touch her, to tell her he was sorry, but he couldn't. He thought about when he first met her, the passion she had aroused in him, how she had brought back romance in his life. The urge to apologise surged up in him again, but he felt restrained, unemotional. He didn't know why. She reminded him so much of Sirra whom he had left behind in Menamo—pristinely beautiful but obstinate, single-minded, and unpredictable. He always imagined the kind of upbringing he would provide for Kevin if his legs had been normal. Yes, he had sent him to one of the best schools in Yaoundé; but he would have loved to take him to the park, go shopping with him, pick him up from school in his car. *Général* turned the chair and wheeled it furiously towards the front door. He turned round and looked at Martina momentarily.

"Martina," he said in a voice that did not sound like his own. "Martina. I'm ... I'm ... I shouldn't have slapped you." He tried to say he was sorry, but the words could not come out. They were stuck somewhere inside his ambivalent self. Strong floods of nostalgic tears began welling up in him. He fought hard to subdue them. He had the strong feeling that if he did not leave the room the tears would surface and unravel the multiple contradictions and complexities of his twisted life. He opened the door quickly and called out to the men in the hidden car. Mokolo and Etoudi came up to the front landing and carried the wheelchair down the stairs.

Martina stood up and walked to the front door. She banged it shut and turned the key in the lock. She heard the car start and drive away. Then she walked to the wall switch and put out the lights in the living room.

ELEVEN

Bosco and Gaston were drenched in sweat as they pulled the wheelchair up the never-ending flight of stairs at the Ministry of Public Service. It was already 8:40 AM. People going up and down the stairs looked at them with questioning glances. There was an expression of disgust on *Général*'s face as he surveyed the traffic of people going up and down the floors of the ministry. Gaston was tall and huge with an angular face. Bosco was stocky. His head was clean shaven, smooth and shinny as if it was rubbed with oil. He wore dark glasses. Gaston glanced up briefly as they came up to the landing on the fifth floor.

When they reached the eighth floor, *Général* asked them to take a rest while they waited for him. He rolled the wheelchair along the corridor and began looking for Room 814D. When he finally saw it, he opened the door without knocking and found himself in a spacious office. A young woman in her late twenties was sitting on a swivel chair behind a large office desk on which there was a flat screen monitor. She was on the phone when *Général* came in. He looked around and noticed four other men sitting on less comfortable chairs. After a while, she put down the phone and turned round. She looked at the *Général*.

"*Oui Monsieur*," she said, "can I help you?" Her attitude was nonchalant, almost condescending.

"I'd like to see Mr. Assuma," *Général* said.

"Have you got an appointment, *Monsieur*?"

"No."

She looked at him in disgust and said, "I'm sorry, you have to take an appointment. The director is in a meeting. All these men are waiting to see him. You have to book an appointment for tomorrow. The director is too busy to receive you today. Can I have your name?"

Général smiled to himself. "I don't have time to come here tomorrow, and I'm not used to waiting." He pulled out a visiting card from his shirt pocket and gave it to the secretary.

The woman took the card and looked at it with amusement. "*Général?*"

"Yes. Pick up the phone and tell him *Général* wants to see him now."

"I told you he was in a meeting—"

Général was already wheeling the chair towards the padded door that led to the director's office. He stopped for a moment when the woman picked up the phone.

"There's a man here who is pushing his way into your office ... No, sir ... In a wheelchair ... *Général* ... Yes, I mean no ... Yes, sir ... Okay." The woman put down the phone. There was an expression of disdain on her face. She stood up and opened the padded door. "You can go in." There was a faint cynical smile on *Général's* face as he entered the office. Assuma stood up at once as *Général* wheeled himself into the spacious office. He closed the door as soon as *Général* came in. He wore a dark suit and his dark angular face was contorted in anger. His lips trembled as he spoke.

"I warned you never to come to my office," his voiced quavered, as he pointed his index finger at *Général*. "What do you want here so early in the morning?"

"You know why I'm here," *Général* said as he looked at the small fridge, the thick red carpet, the heavy curtains, the ebony carvings, the stacks of files on the floor, and the Italian leather furniture. "And will you stop shouting. It doesn't befit a man in your position. It will only irritate me."

"This is not the place for us to talk about rents," the director replied. "I'm supposed to be dealing with your housing agent." Despite the air conditioning in the room, he was sweating.

Général turned the chair slightly and rolled it towards the director's desk. "Look here, Mr. Assuma. Listen carefully to what I'm saying. I'm not here to play word games with you. You owe me six months' rents. Every month you come up with one excuse or another. That's why I'm here."

Assuma took a deep breath and sighed wearily. He stood up, came out from behind his office desk and took off his coat. He threw it on another table and loosened his tie. Then he took out a handkerchief from his pocket and wiped his perspiring brow. He began pacing his office as he addressed *Général*.

"What do you want me to do?" he asked in utter exasperation. "What I receive as salary does not match my monthly needs. I can't make ends meet. How do you expect me to pay the rents for your house?"

"Go out in the streets and join the teachers and medical doctors who want this new parliament to prosecute the big men who have embezzled the nation's money. Join the protests in the streets and march with those who want increases in salaries."

"You have no right to talk to me in my office like this."

"I have a right to my rents."

"My God, you're a very difficult man. What do you want me to do? Go and hold up a bank? Steal money? Many years ago, as director, I had everything—"

"Forget about your past glories. It's people like you who have ruined this country. Fake allowances, inflated budgets from which money was stolen and sent to foreign accounts. Your selfish lifestyle has ruined this—"

"Stop it! That's enough!" the director shouted at the top of his voice. "You have no right to come to my office and talk to me like this. How did you acquire your wealth? You ride a luxurious

Mercedes car. You're chauffeur-driven. You own houses all over the city. Tell me how you made your money?"

"From begging," the disabled man replied. "I'm a beggar, you know."

"And since when have beggars been having choices in this country, criticising the government, and forcing their way into the office of top civil servants?"

"I no longer hear the voice of a man who owes me six months' rents," *Général* said. "Very well then, let me tell you. I've already made up my mind."

"What do you mean made up your mind?"

Général stared him hard on the face. "Today is the twenty-eighth. You have exactly forty-eight hours to get out of my house. You can keep the rents for the six months you haven't paid. But you must get out of the house after tomorrow."

The director walked towards him. "Is this some kind of joke? Get out of the house? In two day's time? Are you crazy? You'll have to give me one or two months to quit the house."

Général rolled the wheelchair away from the director, towards the window. He parted the curtains and looked through the window at the cars in the parking lot below. He let his eyes stray to the Central Lake in the distance. Then he turned round and looked at the director.

"In that case, I'll get your things thrown out. I already have a new tenant for the house."

"Throw my things out?" The director laughed scornfully. "What right have you got to do that? What law gives you that power? Go ahead, do it and you'll pay for it. The housing agreement I signed stipulated one month advance notice, either way. Your action will be a breach of contract. This is a matter for the police. There must be a probe about your wealth. You have no right to—"

"Did I hear you mention the police?" *Général* asked. "That sounds like a threat. You threaten me because of my rents?"

"I'm afraid you have to leave my office right now," the director said sternly. "I have a lot of work to do. I'll prefer not to deal with you any longer. You have a housing agent who's supposed to handle your rents. Henceforth, I'll deal with him directly. And now, will you leave my office?"

Général reflected for a few moments before he turned the wheelchair. He went back again to the window and parted the curtains. He looked at the lake below. He pondered briefly about its tranquillity before turning round to face the director.

"Do you ever have time to look through this window, to look at the still waters of the lake?"

"You're wasting my time."

"It's such a placid lake," *Général* said. "It's so calm, so serene. Come and have a look."

"Get out of my office!"

Général let the curtains drop. He rolled the wheelchair towards the padded door. Assuma held the door open.

"You've refused to come to the window, to see how calm the lake is. A man like you should admire the beauty of nature. In any case, I feel quite sorry for you. You've just thrown a dirty stone in the middle of a calm lake."

The director banged the door shut as *Général* went. He pushed the wheelchair out into the corridor and propelled it towards the direction where Bosco and Gaston where waiting for him.

* * *

They brought Idris Aldabi to the container at about 7:45 PM on Saturday night. He stood almost two meters tall with broad square shoulders and an aggressive jaw-line. He appeared to have already taken a lot of beating. His shirt was stained with blood, and the jean trousers he wore were torn and covered in mud. His face was bruised and his lips were cut and swollen; his right eye was closed. The sagging bags underneath his eyes were puffed with black spots. Bright red blood trickled down his left nostril. Bosco and Gaston supported him on both arms. Idris bent his head and shoulders as Gaston and Bosco shoved him into the container. He stumbled and barely stopped himself from falling down. Mokolo, Etoudi, and the rest of *Général's* men came in after Bosco and Gaston. The boy in charge of Mvog-Mbi was the last to step into the container. The men sat down, one after another. Bosco and Gaston stood on both sides of Idris Aldabi. *Général* was reading when Idris was brought in. He was comfortably reclined in his wheelchair behind the table. A wry smile was faintly visible on his face when Idris was bundled into the container.

"It's good to see you again, *Monsieur* Aldabi," *Général* said. "It's a long time since we met face to face. A very long time."

"What do you want with me?" Idris said. He spoke with visible pain on his face.

"You just came out of prison," *Général* said in a matter-of-fact voice.

"What about it? Is this why your men should beat me up like this?"

Général looked round at the faces of his men before he spoke to Idris. "I'm quite sorry they had to use force to bring you here. It was not intentional, I assure you."

"Well, what is it? Why have your men brought me here? Tell me what you want. You're no longer playing by the rules—"

"The rules have not changed," *Général* responded. "We had an established order before you went to Kondengui. But you broke that order as soon as you came out. You should have let us know that you were out. Why did you have to go into hiding? What little ideas did you hatch out while you were serving your term?"

There was a cynical, defiant expression on Aldabi's swollen face. "Who gave you the power to decide what goes on in this city? We all created the order. No one has the right to administer the order alone."

An insidious smile appeared on *Général*'s face. He moved the wheelchair and came out from behind the table. He came close to Aldabi and looked up at the man's towering frame. "Before you went to Kondengui, Mvog-Mbi was my territory. You had your territory. We all had our territories. Those were the rules. How come your men have moved into Mvog-Mbi?"

"I lost all my territory while I was in prison. It was carved out to other controllers. I had to do something when I came out."

"I was not involved in the division of your territory when you were in prison," *Général* said. "The other controllers didn't even inform me. I only heard of it, much later."

"But you already have too much territory. What do you want? The whole city?"

"I deserve it."

"Why? Tell me why? Who gives you the power to control people's lives, to get me bloodied by these animals you keep around here?"

Without any warning, Aldabi lunged at the wheelchair and threw himself on *Général*. The chair toppled over and the two men crashed on the floor. The men in the container were momentarily taken aback. But they swung into action. Bosco, Gaston, and two other men fell on Aldabi. One man gave him a punch on his abdomen, another drove a fist into his ribs. Idris groaned twice and let go of the wheelchair. Two other men rushed to *Général*. His reading glasses had fallen off during the scuffle. The men straightened the chair and put *Général* back into it. Aldabi received four more blows on his stomach and chest. *Général* raised up his hand.

"Enough," he said. "We don't want to kill him."

Aldabi spat on the floor as blood oozed from his mouth. "You ... you whld bstsh ... you whld pay for this." His words were hardly audible.

"I hear you have also moved into the *zoua zoua* market. That was, and is still under my sole control. You knew that before you were incarcerated."

Aldabi spat out more blood mixed with spittle. His was more audible this time. "I had to survive!" he said. "What did you want me to do?"

Bosco and Gaston twisted his arms and forced him to kneel down in front of *Général*. Aldabi tried to resist.

"Come on, kneel down!" Bosco hissed between his teeth. He was still panting from the brief struggle to overcome Aldabi.

Général held up his hand again. "We can't force him. He knows the rules. Let him take his time. It's his choice."

For two or three minutes, no one uttered a word. Everyone stared at Aldabi. Reluctantly, he went down on his knees and stayed there.

"Pick up *Général*'s glasses!" Gaston commanded him.

Aldabi picked up the glasses and handed them to *Général*. *Général* brought out a white handkerchief from his pocket, wiped the glasses carefully before he put them back on his face.

"Well, go on," Mokolo said. "You know the old ritual. We don't have to remind you—"

"I've told you not to hurry him up. It must come from him. He knows the rules." *Général* rolled the wheelchair and went back to his former position behind the office table.

Idris looked around him again. The defiance on his swollen face gradually gave way to a look of submission and compliance. Slowly, he lowered his forehead and let it touch the floor. He raised his head and repeated the gesture twice. He tried to rise, but Bosco and Gaston held him down.

"It's okay," *Général* ordered them. There was an expression of triumphant satisfaction on his face. "Leave him alone. He can stand up by himself." Aldabi stood up.

"Just like old times," *Général* said, "just like old times. Things haven't changed much, you know. You can't change the order by yourself. And for the second part of the ritual. You know it quite well. Under the bridge, where the train passes. By the railway line."

"No," Aldabi pleaded. "That will be too much. You've already humiliated me. Look at what your men have done to me."

"They will be more lenient this time. We all established the rules. I have no choice."

"No," Aldabi pleaded again.

"Yes. You're lucky it's not a direct confrontation with the 10 PM train from Douala. You will not live to recall the memory. Take him away!" *Général* ordered his men.

"Okay, let's go," the youth in charge of Mvog-Mbi said. Bosco and Gaston grabbed Idris on both arms.

Aldabi tried to shake them off. "No," he pleaded, "I've already suffered a lot. Let me go."

"Before you leave ...," *Général* began. Aldabi turned his head. "I'll let you sell *zoua zoua*. But we will distribute it to you. For nine months. One hundred and fifty francs below our wholesale price. The market is good, and it's getting better. That will allow you make some profit and help you put your life back. Mvog-Mbi is still under my jurisdiction. We'll have to relocate you to some other part of the city. I will arrange it, but it will take time. You'll eventually recover your old territory. No one breaks the rules."

Aldabi swallowed hard and tried to say something, but the men hurried him out. Before the last man left the container, *Général* said to him, "Don't be too hard on him. He's better off alive than dead. He's got a wife and three children. Don't forget to tell the other men."

When they left, *Général* reflected on his life and activities in Yaoundé. The more he descended into evil, the less he could tap into the pool of supernatural power he had acquired after his coma. In the early years after he came out of the coma, he had devoted himself and his mystical power to help people—heal disorders, cure diseases, trace lost relatives, and warn people of impending danger. But as the years passed, the glamour and materialism of the city became alluring. The money he earned as a seer and healer had become inadequate for his ever-growing needs. Today he was no longer the seer he used to be. Some of his skills were there but he was gradually degenerating into a charlatan, swindling the unwary of their money. He knew the mysterious power that had redeemed him from the viciousness of the city would one day disappear if at all it hadn't already done so. Now he relied on his network of human agents and contacts—who were his eyes and ears—to know who came to Yaoundé, who was leaving, who had died, the latest government rumours, and even imminent cabinet reshuffles.

He remembered the dream in which he met his deceased father. In the dream, his father looked like an older version of himself.

"Who are you?" he asked the man, not quite certain whether it was his father or not. "Why do you look like me?"

His father's voice had not changed after all these years in death. "In the spiritual world we can take any shape, or any form," his father replied. "I may look like you, but I'm your father. Am I not in you and you in me?"

"What do you want with me? You died a long time ago."

"And what about you, you also died a long time ago."

"No, I'm alive!" he said vehemently. "I'm alive!"

"Alive? What about your mother? What about Sirra, Pa Wat-echi's daughter who you were supposed to marry? What about your brother, Fabian? You're dead to them." Akuma bowed his head in humiliation. "But you can live again, Akuma," his father had said. "You can regain your life."

"I can't, father. How can I? Look! Look at these stumps that were once my legs."

"Stumps?" his father said incredulously. "What stumps? What are you talking about?"

He looked down. To his amazement, he was no longer sitting in a wheelchair. He was standing up erect. "This can't be true," he said to himself. "I can't believe it."

"It's true," his father had said, "it's true. You just have to believe in yourself that you're alive. It's in your mind."

"I can't believe it," he'd said again.

"You have to believe it," his father insisted. "You could have been a lawyer or a magistrate. You could have gone into politics, become a Member of Parliament, a director in any ministry, or a government minister. You could have become anything. You're quite gifted and intelligent."

He bowed his head in shame.

"But you've brought shame to yourself and the family name. Shame to yourself. Disgrace! Shame! Disgrace! Shame! Shame—"

It was at that moment that he woke up. His heart was pounding heavily against his chest and he was covered in sweat. Why would his dead father appear to him in a dream and look like himself? What did the dream mean? He rolled himself round, reached for the light switch by the bedside and put on the bedside light. He looked at the time on the wall clock. It was 3.30 AM

TWELVE

The pensioner came back to see *Général* on Wednesday evening. He was in a light-hearted mood as he walked towards the container. *Général* was attending to two women and a man when he came. He asked the pensioner to take a walk around Anguissa and come back in about half an hour.

When he came back forty-five minutes later, the people were gone. *Général* was alone in the container. He looked up as the pensioner came in.

"What happened? Did you see the *préfet*?"

"Yes, I did." The pensioner was obviously excited. "All the documents have been certified. When I got there, his secretaries told me he was too busy to see anyone. And it was already 10 AM. He was getting ready to attend a political rally."

"But I gave you a note to give him. You had it on you. You should have insisted—"

"I did. They looked me over and asked me why I wanted to see him. I told them it was personal and urgent. Then I remembered the note you gave me. I told them I had a letter for the *préfet*. One of the girls—so many secretaries in one office—one of the girls, the most beautiful one asked me to give her the letter. They didn't even offer me a chair. She took the letter in and came out immediately. She ushered me into the *préfet*'s office."

Général smiled. "Well?"

"He asked me whether I was a friend of yours. When I said I was, he said he was quite glad to make my acquaintance. He stamped all the documents with the official seal, signed them, and gave them back to me."

Général laughed aloud. "Man-know-man! That's how people get contracts, how appointments are made. A minister, rector or director, knows a man from his tribe or his village and gives him a contract, recommends him for a top appointment. That's how the regime works."

"I was quite surprised," the pensioner went on. "He didn't even ask who I was, my name, that kind of thing. He didn't ask for the originals of the documents he was certifying. And it didn't take me up to five minutes."

"Do you have them here with you?"

The pensioner reached into his raffia bag and brought out a big envelope. "Do I take them back to Public Service?"

"Give them to me. I'll send them there myself. I have my own channels. I'll use my contacts there to accelerate the pace of the dossier. If you follow the regular route, it will take another three or four months before the ministerial decision on your pension comes out."

The pensioner handed *Général* the envelope. "You're quite certain all the documents are here, your latest pay voucher too?"

"Yes, everything is in there. I ... I do not..." the pensioner hesitated.

"Did you say something?"

"Yes," the pensioner said. "I wonder, I wonder. Why ... Why are you doing all this for me? I'm a total stranger to you. What makes you do this?"

For a few moments, *Général* did not say anything. He became slightly agitated as he wiped his nose with the fingers of his left hand. He could not look the pensioner directly in the face. Why was he helping the old man?

Deep inside him he knew why, but he could not bring the real reason for what appeared to be good intentions to the surface.

He reflected on what the city had done to him a long time ago when he first came to Yaoundé. Yaoundé was merciless, callously brutal to unwary and naive young men like himself who came to the metropolis, unsuspecting that the city had its own code of conduct—unwritten laws that had to be obeyed. There were no saints and sinners in a system like this. You were either a prey or a predator. He looked at the old man and wondered how he could tell him that the city had turned him into a predator.

"Is anything wrong?" the pensioner asked. "Did I say something improper?"

"No," *Général* said. "No. You've asked me a very difficult question. I don't know what to say. I ... I didn't know I'll eventually confront this part of myself. The reason I do what I'm doing."

"But why?" The pensioner appeared surprised. "It makes you a good man."

"How dare you say I'm a good man?" *Général* retorted harshly. "You hardly know me."

"But look at what you've done for me. How you've helped me. Without you, I would have been moving around in circles."

"How much do you expect from your pension arrears?" *Général* demanded.

"I don't know. I tried to calculate a rough estimate the other day. About eight million francs."

"That's a lot of money for an old man," *Général* said. "What are you going to do with it?"

"I already told you. I have an uncompleted house in the village and a large extended family. My children are still in secondary school. But what has this got to do with your generosity, your willingness to help."

"Let's not talk about this any longer," *Général* said.

The old man wondered why *Général* could not look at him as they spoke. He was restless, fidgeting with papers, pens, stamp pads, and other things on his table, not focussing his attention on anything in particular. The disabled man turned the wheelchair round and began searching the bookcase for something.

The pensioner cleared his throat. "How long do you think I'll wait before the decision comes out?"

"About a week," *Général* said. He was still busy, looking for something on the shelf. "I will use all my contacts at Public Service to ensure the decision comes out in about a week. After that, the dossier will be forwarded to the Ministry of Finance."

"Well, in that case, I still have about two more weeks to spend in Yaoundé."

"Don't limit yourself to any time frame. Give yourself another month or so. I know it's difficult for you, living with relatives, and the little money you brought getting diminished everyday." *Général's* back was still turned on the old man.

"I'll like to go now," the pensioner said. "I need to go home and rest. I've been on my feet all day." *Général* did not answer. The pensioner walked out of the container quietly. He followed the path that led to the street in front of *Rio bar d'Anguissa*.

He thought about why *Général* had behaved so oddly. Why did he say he was not a good man? Did it have something to do with his consultations, his ability to see into the past and the future? Why did *Général* not look at him directly in the face this evening? He decided to go straight home. He walked down to the bar and turned right at the Anguissa intersection. As he turned round to look behind, he saw a blue Toyota police van drive down the street. It stopped directly opposite the *Rio bar d'Anguissa*. Five policemen trooped out of the van and headed in the direction of *Général's* headquarters.

* * *

Frederic Onana, the Superintendent in charge of the Seventh District police station, his assistant, Inspector Manuel Nana and three other policemen in uniform knocked on the container and walked in without waiting for an answer. It was close to 7:30 PM.

Général was unmistakably surprised by the sudden appearance of the policemen. He knew the police Superintendent and the Inspector. He had not seen the other constables before.

"Well, well, *mon Commissaire*. What a surprise." *Général* glanced at his business licence. "A thought crossed my mind that perhaps I had forgotten to pay my taxes to the government. But as you can see the licence is not yet expired."

"We're not from taxation," Superintendent Onana said. "You know who we are."

"And for what reason, if I may ask, do I deserve this visit? This is rather too sudden, you must admit. You should have sent word you were coming. I should have sent for red wine or champagne."

"Enough of that!" the Superintendent cut in sharply. "None of your twisted sense of humour this night. Tell us what you know about Philip Assuma. He was your tenant."

"*Was*? He *is* still my tenant. What about him?"

The Superintendent and Inspector glanced at each other. "You visited him about a week ago. In his office," the Inspector said.

"I did, yes."

The Superintendent brought out a notebook and began taking notes. "What was the purpose of your visit?"

"Had you visited him before? Had you ever been to his office?" Inspector Nana added.

"Hey, wait a minute. What's all this about? Is this an interrogation?"

"Don't tell us you don't know what has happened," the Inspector said.

"Well, you tell me."

The two officers looked at each other again. The Superintendent said, "Philip Assuma is dead! He was found floating in the Central Lake three days ago. We're investigating the circumstances surrounding his death. It was quite sudden and unexpected."

"And what makes you come here?" There was a note of sarcasm in *Général's* voice.

"He was your tenant. And he owed you six months of unpaid rents. That we know, for sure," Superintendent Onana said.

"And what do you not know?" *Général* demanded.

"Whether you have a hand in his death," Inspector Nana said.

Général turned his head from the Inspector and looked at the Superintendent. "What will I benefit from his death? He was more useful to me alive than dead. At least, he owed me six months rents. That's a lot of money in these difficult times."

"We're just gathering useful information," the Superintendent said. "Two other details. Idris Aldabi was found some days ago tied with ropes and left by the railway line, underneath the bridge at Olezoa."

"He's quite lucky the train didn't crush him to death," Inspector Nana said. "But his face was badly mutilated. His left cheek was slashed with some sharp instrument, probably a knife. What do you know of this incident?"

"Nothing."

"Nothing?" The Inspector looked surprised. "But that's the ritual of settling scores among you people. What do you mean nothing?"

"Listen, Idris just came out of prison six months ago. Several gangs have sprung all over the city. Whose fault is it? Mine? Soldiers and policemen are sponsoring robberies almost every week. Shoot outs between armed robbers and the police have increased over the last year. Stolen and unregistered guns are everywhere. The city has become totally unsafe," *Général* said.

"The government, the police, you people have lost control of everything. Idris Aldabi is an ex-convict. You know him better than I do. A lot of people may have old scores to settle with him. What has it got to do with me? I think you've come to the wrong place," *Général* concluded. "And what about the second detail. I'm quite busy, as you can see."

"Some tourists lost their passports to pickpockets in Mokolo market. Can you give us a clue, any help?" Superintendent Onana asked.

Général turned the wheelchair and opened one of the boxes behind him. He brought out four passports— American, Dutch, German, and British—and gave them, one after the other, to the Superintendent. "Is this what you're looking for?"

"At least, we're not wrong here," the Superintendent said. There was a vague, conspiratory smile on his face. "I told the Inspector we could always count on you."

The initial hostility with which *Général* had received them suddenly changed. "I'm always willing to help you when you come here with the right attitude."

When the Superintendent spoke again, his voice had lost its authoritative tone. He was now more relaxed and friendly. The Inspector and the other policemen too were less tense and rigid. "Before we go—" the Superintendent began. He looked around and hesitated. He ordered the three constables to go back to the van on the road and wait for the Inspector and himself.

After they had left, he continued, "Before we go, the Inspector and I would like to buy some *zoua zoua* for our cars."

"I thought senior police officers got free fuel at the Longkak National Security Headquarters," *Général* said. "You know I only supply wholesale."

"We know. But you have to help us," the Inspector pleaded. "The free pumps at Longkak have been restricted to the top brass in the police and special branch. We've been excluded. Part of the belt-tightening measures government has taken to fight the economic crisis."

"I see," *Général* said. "How much do both of you need?"

"Two, one hundred litre drums. One each, for both of us," the

Superintendent said.

"That's a lot of gasoline. I will sell it to you at the retail price."

"Come on, Général," Inspector Nana said, "these are hard times. Leave the two drums for us at the wholesale price. We can pay for that."

Général reflected for a moment. "My stock is a bit low now. Can you come in three day's time? I expect fresh deliveries from Bakassi. I'll get you the two drums."

The Superintendent glanced at his watch and turned to the Inspector. "It's been a busy and fruitful night. We better get moving."

"Well, Général," Inspector Nana said, "we'll be seeing you."

"It was good to see you again," Général said. When the two men left, he brought out a big map of the city, spread it on his table, and began studying it. When he finished examining the map, he took his cell phone and dialed Mvog-Mbi's number. The number was busy. He called the number again after five minutes. It was still busy. Ten minutes later, he received a 'bip me' message from Mvog-Mbi. He dialed the number again and heard it ringing.

"Yes, Général?"

"Where are you?"

"In Emana, Général."

"What are you doing in Emana?"

"Visiting my girlfriend, Général.

"How soon can you be here?" Général inquired.

"Is it urgent, Général?"

"Yes, very urgent!"

"In twenty minutes, Général, if that's okay with you."

"Okay, be here in twenty minutes then," Général said as he switched off the line.

Twenty minutes later Mvog-Mbi knocked on the container door. Général said, "It's open. Come in."

As soon as Mvog-Mbi entered the container Général said,

"Where's the bike? Has it been repaired?"

"I couldn't find the original parts, *Général*, but I found used ones from Belgium."

"You didn't tell me."

"I forgot, *Général*."

"How much do the parts cost? Did you find out?"

"Fifty-eight thousand, five hundred francs."

"And the labour for repairing the bike?"

"Should not be more than ten thousand, *Général*."

Général rolled the wheelchair towards the table and opened a drawer. "Here's sixty thousand," he said. "I want the bike fixed tomorrow."

"As you say, *Général*." He turned to depart.

"Before you go," *Général* said, "I'm giving you a temporary reassignment from your usual part of the city. You will suspend all activities in Mvog-Mbi until further notice."

"Yes, *Général*."

"It's about the old man, the one I'm helping to get his pension arrears. I am re-assigning you to keep an eye on him every day, all day, till he's paid his pension arrears at the treasury."

"I'm listening, *Général*."

"Follow him on your bike on the day he is paid his arrears. Keep a good distance behind him. And for God's sake wear your helmet. I don't want you to be identified. Unscrew the bike's licence plates, front and back."

"What if he takes a taxi?"

"I don't think he will. He's too cautious. He will avoid taking a taxi at all costs. But if he does, stay close behind the taxi, until he comes out. You understand?"

"I understand, *Général*."

"He will likely put the entire amount of the arrears money in his raffia bag, the one he carries around with him everywhere. I want you to get the bag."

"I'll do as you say, *Général*."

"It will be ideal to avoid a scuffle with the old man in the street. That will attract attention and you may be identified. You need some kind of distraction. I wonder how you'll do it."

Mvog-Mbi thought for a while. After a few moments, he said, "I'll get in touch with a gang of street boys in Mvog-Ada and arrange something. I've worked with them before. I'll pay each of them a thousand francs to create a scene, something in the street that will distract the old man."

"Good. I'll change my closing hours until he's paid the money at the Treasury. I will stay here every day until 9 PM. When you get the bag come immediately to the container. I know how much money will be in the raffia bag."

"Is that all, *Général*?"

"No, that's not all. I've figured out what plot you may be hatching. You're thinking this could be your lucky break. Forget it. I've taken all necessary precautions, a back-up plan, just in case you intend to escape with the money." *Général*'s voice took an abrasive tone. "From now on, the moment you leave this place, you will be followed. You won't see who because you won't know who. But they'll monitor you, day and night. You'll be shot dead the moment you decide to escape with the money. Do I make myself clear?"

"You don't have confidence in me, *Général*?"

"I don't have confidence in anybody," *Général* said sternly, "not even in myself. You can go now."

Mvog-Mbi walked out of the container and closed the door behind him.

THIRTEEN

When the pensioner next visited him, *Général* was distant and cheerless. The smile that used to be on his face, and the usual wit and jokes that characterised the pensioner's visits to the container had disappeared. He didn't seem to pay any particular attention to the old man when he entered the container that Wednesday evening. He brought out an envelope and handed it to the pensioner.

"Here's a photocopy of your *arrêté*, the ministerial ordinance from Public Service. It came out a week ago. I think they've already forwarded it to Finance."

The pensioner took the envelope. *Général*'s face was had an inscrutable expression. He glanced at the pensioner briefly. The pensioner tried to study *Général*'s face in an attempt to detect any clue about the man's sudden transformation. *Général* looked indifferent.

"Take note of the reference. You'll have to follow the file at Finance yourself. I've become very busy—"

"You've already done quite a lot—"

"The route your file will follow at Finance is fairly straightforward. You may have to spend a little bit of money—"

"I'll come back and see you when I get the money. I'll like to show how grateful I—"

"You don't have to come back here or give me anything." *Général*'s tone was brusque and snappy. "I may be travelling. You'll not meet me if you come here next week."

The old man stared at *Général*. He was puzzled. He didn't know what to say. He stood up and began putting away the envelope in the raffia bag.

"I'm sorry," *Général* said. "If we don't see each other before you collect your arrears, I wish you a safe trip back to your hometown."

The old man didn't say another word. He stepped out of the container and walked away in the direction of the *Rio bar d'Anguissa*.

The following day was a Tuesday. The pensioner went to the Ministry of Finance at 8 AM. He met someone at the back entrance of the ministry who directed him to go to R-25. *Service de Titre Réglements* was written on the door of R-25. He went inside and asked one of the workers about the procedure of following up pension files.

"We don't treat pension files here," the man told him. "You have to go to Room 214. It's on the second floor."

The pensioner climbed the stairs slowly until he came to the second floor. He walked down a narrow corridor and saw 214 on a door. He read the inscription on the door. *Direction de la Solde: Service de Pension.* The room had three tables. The first one was occupied by a man and the other two by women. One of the women, a lady in her early forties, looked up from the work she was doing as the pensioner came in.

"*Oui?*" she said. "Do you want anything, *Monsieur?*"

"My pension papers. I don't know where to begin."

"You have to go to *Renseignement*, Room 218," the woman said.

When the pensioner got to Room 218, he found another woman at the information desk. This one was much younger and sympathetic.

"Were you with the territorial administration, the army, or the civil service?" the young woman asked him.

"With Secondary Education," the pensioner said. "I was a principal."

"In that case, *Monsieur*, you have to go down to the *Courrier Central* to verify whether your file has been dispatched to this ministry. That is where you have to start."

"And where would that be?" the pensioner asked.

"Outside this main administrative block, opposite the Ministry of Agriculture."

The pensioner went downstairs and came out of the ministry. The central mail service unit was opposite the Ministry of Agriculture, as the woman had said. There was a young woman seated at the reception. The pensioner walked up and greeted her before he said, "I'm searching for my pension file."

"Do you have the reference of the *arrêté* from the Public Service?" the young woman asked him.

The pensioner brought out the envelope *Général* had given him from his raffia bag. He removed the photocopied decision from the envelope and handed it to the woman. The woman took the decision, entered his name and registration number in the computer in front of her, and began searching for the pensioner's reference.

"Here it is," the woman said. She looked for a piece of paper and scribbled the reference number and a date on it. She gave the pensioner the paper. "It was dispatched to *Courrier Solde*," the woman said. "All dossiers and letters that have to do with pensions are sent there as soon as they get here. We only sort out the mail."

She handed the pensioner the piece of paper. "This is your reference, and the date your file left this section. You should use this piece of paper. You don't have to bring out a copy of your *arrêté* every time to show the reference."

"Thank you very much," the pensioner said. "You've been so helpful." The woman nodded and smiled.

When the pensioner got to *Courrier Solde*, the man who searched for his reference told him that his file had already been forwarded to Room 214. The pensioner climbed the stairs to the second floor and went again to Room 214. He gave the new reference on the piece of paper to the elderly woman.

"*Oui?*" the woman said, as she took the piece of paper.

"I was here a while ago," the pensioner said.

"*Mais oui,*" the woman said. "You found the reference, I see. We can't trace people's dossiers without these references. There're so many people and so many files."

She flipped through a thick register as she spoke. When she located the pensioner's reference, she looked up. "Here it is. I'll have to find out whether the director has approved and signed it. She went to an old dusty cabinet and began rearranging stacks of files. She brought back a bunch of files and began flipping through them.

"I don't seem to find your file. But our entry register shows that it arrived here." She stood up and entered the director's office. After a while, she came out. "Your file is not on his desk. He signed all of them this morning."

"Could the file be missing?" the pensioner wondered.

"No," the woman said. "Not in this office. We've not had a missing or lost file here for the past three months. Wait a minute," she said with some sudden inspiration. "How much money are you expecting?"

"About eight million francs."

"*Mon Dieu!* That's a lot of money. Now I see. Your file is not missing. It's gone up to the minister's secretariat. My boss is only authorized to approve amounts of less than five million francs. Anything above that has to receive the minister's authorisation."

"I see."

"Why don't you come back here after tomorrow? The file should have come down here by then, I assure you." She closed the register, stood up, and took the bunch of files back to the cabinet. When she came back, he thanked her and walked out of the room.

The pensioner came back to the Ministry on Wednesday morning. He went straightaway to Room 214. The woman recognised him as soon as he walked into the room.

"*Bonjour, Madame.*"

"*Bonjour, Monsieur.* Your file descended yesterday evening. I have it here with me." She showed the old man a chair and opened a drawer. She brought out a file and put it on her table. "This is it," she said, as she looked through the first pages of the file. "The minister has already approved the arrears. Here're his stamp and signature."

"What happens now?" the old man demanded. "Where does the dossier go to after this?"

The woman laughed. "You must forgive me, *Monsieur.* But I'm not laughing at you. Is this your first time in this ministry?"

"Yes."

"The file keeps on going up and down the ministry. The owner of the file is obliged to follow it up and down the building, to every office it goes, to ensure someone in that service treats it and does not leave it lying on a table or hidden in a drawer. If you leave the file and think your arrears will be paid, you may have to wait for a whole year or even two."

"Well, in that case, what do I do?"

"You're an old man," the woman said sympathetically. "Going up and down these stairs will exhaust you. And it's not good for a man of your age. You have to look for someone to help you follow the file."

"But I don't know anyone in the ministry."

It doesn't matter," the woman said. "There are professional file chasers all over the ministry. We call them *hommes à tout faire.*"

"Ah, odd job men," the pensioner said.

"Yes, yes, job odd men," the woman laughed with visible enthusiasm in her voice. "Mostly office messengers with low salaries. Before the salary cuts and the devaluation, they used to receive *primes de rendement.* This used to discourage them from taking bribes. But the *primes* too were cut from their salaries—"

"How do I get in touch with one of them? What do I do?"

"You're from Bamenda, yes?" the woman inquired.

"Yes, from Yambe."

"I can tell from the way you speak your French. There's a boy in the Ministry from Bamenda. He works here on this floor. He's very good at following up dossiers and searching for lost files. His name is *le chasseur*. Everybody knows him in the ministry. He'll require some money, of course."

"How much? I don't have much money left on me," the pensioner complained. "It's more than a month since I arrived here. I didn't anticipate I'll stay here for so long."

"I know what you mean, *Monsieur*. He doesn't take all the money for himself. If you come to an agreement with him, you'll be surprised that your *bon de caisse* will come out in a very short time."

The pensioner heaved a sigh of relief. "Where can I find him?"

The woman turned round to one of the other workers in the room. "*Tu connais où on peut trouver le chasseur?*" (Do you know where we can find *Le Chasseur*?)

"*Mais oui. Il doit se cacher quelque part.*" The man stood up and left the office.

"He's gone to look for him. He'll be back soon," the woman told the pensioner.

"Is that his real name, *le chasseur*?"

"No, no," the woman laughed. "His nickname. I'm sure he has a name. But no one really bothers to know what his real name is any longer."

As they were talking, the man who had gone out returned to the office with a lanky young man of about twenty-eight. He wore a grey tie and a faded, black second-hand coat. The soles of his black shoes were completely worn out.

"Did you want to see me, *Madame* Edimo?"

"Yes. I have a client for you," the woman said, pointing at the pensioner. "He needs a little help with his pension file."

"At what level is the file right now?" he asked.

"It came down to my office yesterday."

Le chasseur grinned. It was a strange kind of laugh. The muscles on the left side of his face moved slightly and pushed the left corner of his mouth in a distorted manner to one side.

"The file has not even begun its journey," he said. He turned his head and looked at the old man for the first time. "It's yours?" he asked.

"Yes," the pensioner said.

"I think you can both go out into the corridor and negotiate the details there," *Madame* Edimo suggested.

The pensioner stood up and followed *le chasseur*. As soon as the old man came out in the corridor and shut the door behind him *le chasseur* began talking to him in French.

"I'm English-speaking," the pensioner said, "and besides, my French is not so good. They told me you're from Bamenda. I'm also from Bamenda, from Yambe."

"Who told you about me? That's not why I came to see you. I was told you have a file—"

"Yes," the old man said, "my pension arrears. I want you to help me. I don't understand the system at all. By the way, what's your name? I mean your real name."

The young man hesitated. "Why do you want to know my name? Names don't matter in this place. I hardly think about my name. It's what I do that matters." He glanced at his watch. "We've already wasted a lot of time. Let me have your reference."

The old man searched through his pockets and brought out the piece of paper the woman in the mail room had given him. He handed it to the young man.

Le chasseur looked at the paper briefly and put it in his shirt pocket before he looked at the pensioner. "The money," he said. "They must have told you."

"How much?"

"Thirty thousand francs."

"Thirty thousand!"

"That's just an advance. I don't start chasing the dossier without the advance."

"And how much do I have to pay you at the end, when everything is finished."

"Twenty thousand francs, just before the dossier gets to the computer service. You don't have to wait until the end. And you pay nothing else."

"Are you telling me you want fifty thousand francs for helping me follow my file from one office to another?"

"I'm not helping you. The money is not for me." He glanced at his watch again. "You're wasting my time."

"Do you know how old I am?" the pensioner asked.

"What?" What has this got to do with—"

A lot of anger had been building up in the old man. It was now surfacing, but *le chasseur* did not realise what was happening. "What did you think I want your name for? To eat it? You've not just been rude to me; you've insulted me as well—"

"Me? Did I insult you?"

"How can you ask me to give you fifty thousand francs to move up and down these stairs? Are you a director? Even directors don't take that much."

"Let me explain. It's not me who'll eat your money—"

"Don't interrupt me when I'm talking. I was once a young man like you, let me tell you. So don't take advantage of my age. Come on, give me back my reference."

"What? You—"

"You heard me. Don't waste my time. Give me the reference."
People who were moving up and down the corridor came nearer when they heard the old man shouting. A small group blocked the corridor as it surrounded the two men.

Le chasseur looked bewildered. He took out the piece of paper from his pocket and gave it back to the old man. He turned round suddenly, elbowed his way through the small crowd and quickly walked down the dimly lit corridor.

The pensioner opened the door of Room 214 and went back into the room. *Madame* Edimo looked up from her work as he came in. "What happened?" she asked.

"I've changed my mind. I've decided to follow the dossier myself."

"*Mais, Monsieur*—"

"*Le chasseur* is a cheat. He wanted to take advantage of my age."

"What a pity, *Monsieur*. This building has five floors. You'll exhaust yourself, going up and down the stairs. At your age."

The pensioner was determined. "I'll follow it myself, even if I collapse on the stairs and die. It's my money."

Madame Edimo shrugged her shoulder. "It's up to you, *Monsieur*. I'll send up the dossier to budget control on the fifth floor this afternoon. The director or his assistant will have to verify and crosscheck the dossier. I advice you to come back tomorrow. If the director doesn't have a lot of work on his table, he'll examine the files and sign them this evening."

"Thank you, *Madame* Edimo. I'll come back tomorrow morning." The pensioner left the room and came out into the corridor. He turned left and walked to the staircase. Then he began descending slowly. He came out at the front entrance of the ministry, the one opposite the Ministry of Health. He glanced at his watch. It was close to eleven thirty. A lot of workers were already leaving the ministry and heading to lunch. He walked through the parking lot and came down to the bus stop beside the ministry. He boarded a taxi that was heading to Anguissa.

The pensioner returned to the Ministry of Finance the next day at 8:30 AM. It took him about ten minutes to reach the fifth floor. He looked up at each door as he walked down the corridor.

Finally, he saw 508D: *Direction du Budget*. He knocked on the door and entered the director's secretariat. A young female secretary sat behind a flat screen monitor. Two men were also seated behind two tables. They all looked bored. The pensioner walked up to one of the men and murmured a greeting.

"*Oui, Monsieur,* what can I do for you?"

The old man brought out his reference and gave it to the man. From his experience at Public Service and in the offices he had entered so far in the Ministry of Finance, he had concluded that workers in these ministries responded to information mechanically, like robots. Any slight departure from their automatic conditioning, like an unnecessary greeting, politeness or a smile, threw them off balance, out of the well-oiled cogs of their mechanical code of conduct.

"What's the file for?" the man asked.

"My pension."

The man pulled a thick black ledger towards him and opened it. He took a quick glance at the reference on the paper and began searching through the ledger. "Ah, here it is. The director signed it yesterday. We've already dispatched it downstairs." He scribbled a reference and a date on the paper and gave it back to the pensioner. "Take it to room 405D. Ask for *Monsieur* Eloundou."

The pensioner went downstairs and found the door quite easily. 405D SD/PB was inscribed on the door. He went in and asked for *Monsieur* Eloundou.

"*Oui*, I'm *Monsieur* Eloundou. What do you want?"

"Someone in Room 508D asked me to see you."

"You have a file then? Let me see your reference. What kind of file is it?"

"It's my pension file," the old man said, as he handed him the reference. Eloundou took the paper and looked at the date the man in 508D had scribbled on it. Then he took a black ledger from his table and began looking for the reference. When he saw it, he looked at the old man.

"Yes," he said. "The file arrived here yesterday. There were more than fifteen files among the lot that came down here. They're all in the director's office. And he's quite busy. I don't think he's signed them. He's not yet come to work this morning. It's still quite early."

"I'll wait," the pensioner said.

"Wait? What for? This director always has a lot of work on his desk. Sometimes he doesn't even look at the files for several days."

"In that case, what do I do?" the pensioner asked Eloundou.

"Come back in two days. We'll see what we can do."

"Two days? That will already be on Thursday."

"And what about it? The director has the final say in this service. Even when your file leaves this office, it must come back here again when your *bon d'engagement* goes upstairs to be signed by the budget director. It's your file that eventually matters, not the number of days or time you spend here."

"I've already spent more than a month in Yaoundé, following this file."

"You can try tomorrow then. Come back here in the afternoon tomorrow. We'll see what we can do."

As the pensioner went out, one of the men in the secretariat followed him out into the corridor. "Can I talk to you, *Monsieur?*" he asked in a low voice. The pensioner turned round and looked at him. "*Monsieur* Eloundou can help you. He can remove your file out of the big pile in the director's office and get it signed by the director, very quickly. He can do it for you. You don't have to give him a lot."

"I understand," the pensioner said. "Can you call him outside for me?" The man went back into the secretariat and Eloundou came out a few moments later.

"*Oui, Monsieur?*"

The pensioner beckoned him to come closer. Then he discreetly slipped five thousand francs in his hand. Eloundou looked at the note briefly and put it away into his pocket. He coughed slightly to clear his throat.

"Come back tomorrow in the afternoon. I'll see what I can do."

The pensioner descended the stairs slowly. His knees were already shaking. He held the handrail on the balustrades as he went down the staircase. His body had begun registering the strain of the tedious climb to the fifth floor. When he came out at the front entrance he took in a deep breath. The air outside and the sunshine were a welcome relief from the musty and dimly lit corridors of the ministry.

The pensioner came back to the ministry again on Wednesday. He took his time climbing the stairs. He rested for a while on the landing of the third floor before he walked up to 405D. There was a smile on Eloundou's face as soon as he saw the old man.

"Sit down, *Monsieur*, sit down," he said, as he showed the pensioner a chair. "I located your dossier. The director has not yet signed it. It's not my fault, you see. But I promise you, he'll do it this afternoon. He's in his office right now. You can wait if you want to. But I advice you to go home. As soon as the director signs it, I'll personally take it next door to 404D so that they prepare your *bon d'engagement*."

"How long will that take?" the pensioner asked him.

"It depends. If there are a lot of files on the desk of the accounts clerk, it might take a while. That's why I want to get out your dossier so that he can work on it quickly," Eloundou explained. "Have you got five thousand francs on you?"

The pensioner dipped his right hand into the raffia bag and brought out a five thousand francs note. There was a shadow of suspicion on his face.

"It's for the man in 404D who will prepare the *bon d'engagement*. This will urge him to work quickly on it. I'll talk to him myself, I assure you."

He handed the money to Eloundou. "What do I do now?"

the pensioner asked.

Eloundou looked at his watch. "Come back tomorrow. It's almost three o'clock. Even if the director signed it at four, it will be too late for the *bon d'engagement* to be prepared today. Come back tomorrow, *Monsieur*."

The pensioner came back to see Eloundou around 10:15 AM on Thursday. The file had made remarkable progress. As soon as the pensioner came in, Eloundou could not hide his feelings. There was an expression of awe and reverence on his face. The pensioner thought something terrible had happened to the file.

"What has happened? Why are you looking at me like that?"

"Do you realise you're a very rich man, *Monsieur*? Your arrears have been calculated. They sent us your *bon d'engagement* for endorsement. It has already been endorsed by the accounts clerk and the chief of service for budget control in 401D. The total sum came up to eight million, eight hundred and fifty thousand francs. That's a lot of money, *Monsieur*!"

"I've not had my pension for seven years since I retired."

"What are you going to do with all that money?" Eloundou asked him.

"I have quite a lot of things to do with it. I have a big extended family and children in school." The pensioner was beginning to feel self-assured. The amount of money on the *bon d'engagement* and the look of respect on Eloundou's face made him feel more confident about himself. "Where's the file now?"

"We've already dispatched it upstairs to the budget director, Room 506. His assistant in Room 502 will also have to countersign it. There's a man in the director's secretariat, an Anglophone. He will be able to help you."

"Did I hear you say an Anglophone? It's not *le chasseur*, is it?" the pensioner asked.

Eloundou laughed. "You know him then, *Monsieur*? *Le chasseur* is a popular fellow here in the ministry."

"I don't want to deal with him," the pensioner said emphatically.

"It's not *le chasseur, Monsieur*. The man in the director's secretariat is called Mokube. He's from Kumba. There are three women and a man in the secretariat. The man sits on the desk to your right, as you open the door. Ask for him when you get there."

The pensioner introduced himself to Mokube as soon as he got to Room 506. They shook hands and Mokube showed offered him a seat.

"Eloundou telephoned me as you were coming up," Mokube said. "You're a very lucky man to have had the arrears of your pension approved."

"It wasn't my fault that the file was held up at Public Service," the pensioner said. "I deserve the money after all these years."

"I understand what you're saying," Mokube said. "That's why I said you're a lucky man indeed. Believe me."

"So where's the file now?"

"It has reached its most crucial stage. All the directors have seen the *bon d'engagement*. That kind of money, that amount, is an invitation for envy, particularly among the directors. They'll use every trick in the book to delay the payment."

"But why, what will it benefit them?"

"Human nature," Mokube said. "You can't blame them. All their allowances have been reduced to nothing. The old privileges of state housing, out of station allowances and so on are gone. Put yourself in their positions. A payment of more than eight million francs falls on your desk. How would you feel?"

"Are all of them that crooked? Is the system totally rotten?"

"It's been ruined beyond redemption. Nothing short of a cataclysm will save it. Most of us are stuck here because we have nowhere else to go. But the surprising thing is that within this spiritless landscape, one still finds a solitary flower struggling to raise its petals above the surface of the disease that's killing the country."

The pensioner did not seem to understand what Mokube was talking about. "What are you talking about?"

"I'm talking about the director in Room 202 who is a born-again Christian. He attends to everyone without thinking of money, or time, or what language a man speaks. It's people like him who deserve to be decorated with medals, not the rotten fellows who apply for them."

The pensioner shrugged his shoulders. "Well, what do I do now?"

"Let me tell you the truth now. I've seen files with big amounts like yours held here for months. A few years ago, you could negotiate with the directors and service chiefs to give them something after you received the money from the treasury. But a lot of people never came back. Now the directors demand raw cash. They want nothing else."

"How much are we talking about here?"

"Anything from a hundred to three hundred thousand. Prepare your mind to spend more money. One can never tell. At this stage, it's a must for one director I know rather well. He'll accept nothing less than a hundred thousand. He calls it money to fuel his car. We also have three service chiefs through whom your file has to pass. And the men in the computer room. You'll have to give them some money too. Without them, the computers can't function."

"*Le chasseur* was right then?" the pensioner reflected.

"*Le chasseur*? How much did he ask you to give him?"

"Fifty thousand francs."

Mokube smiled to himself. "That was a bit too much at his level, but he may have been right after all. You can't blame him. Poverty breeds dishonesty. He has to survive."

"Even if he has to cheat an old man?"

"Poverty has never been a bedfellow with morality," Mokube said. He glanced at his watch. "It will soon be closing time. Do you have the money on you?"

"No, the pensioner replied. "I'll have to get home first."

"In that case, you'll come back tomorrow then."

The old man nodded.

"I'll be waiting for you," Mokube said.

The pensioner returned to the Ministry of Finance the next day at 9 AM. He took his time to climb the stairs. When he got to the fourth floor, his knees were already throbbing with pain. He rested for a while on the landing before he gathered enough strength to make the final climb to the fifth floor. He was breathing heavily and his legs where trembling when he got to Room 506. Mokube felt sorry for him when he walked into his secretariat. He gave him a chair to sit down.

"Pa," Mokube said, "it's too tedious for an old man like you, going up and down these stairs, morning and afternoon. It will wear you down."

"What do you want me to do, my son? Who will do it for me? It's my money, isn't it? Even if I die in the process of getting it, the state will give it to my family. What else can an old man like me hope for?"

"Have you brought the money?"

The pensioner dipped his hand into the raffia bag and brought out three hundred thousand francs. He gave the money to Mokube.

"I've talked to three of the directors this morning who are directly concerned with your file," Mokube said as he took the money. "They're going to help if you understand what I mean."

"What's the next step the file follows once it leaves your boss's office?" the old man asked Mokube.

"Once it leaves here, it goes downstairs again to 405D for the allocated money to be included in the budget. From there it's forwarded to 404D. Thereafter, once the right contacts are made, thanks to this money, things will move pretty fast."

"Does the file come upstairs again?"

"No. It keeps on going downstairs after this. It's taken to room

178

105. That's *Courrier Ordinateur*, the computer mail service room, where it's registered and discharged to the computer service. Once the information on your file is entered into the computer, and the money you are due is budgeted in your name, every other thing after that is just standard bureaucratic procedure."

"What about the cash voucher? When do I get it?"

"The *bon de caisse*? It's not handed to you," Mokube explained. "After it's allocated in the budget, it's finally sent down to the basement in R30, the *Service du Retrait des Bons de Caisse*.

"What does it mean?"

"Something about where the cash vouchers are retrieved. Difficult to translate."

"I see. It sounds as if that's the final stage."

"More or less. Thereafter, it's sent to the treasury for payment."

The old man was visibly impressed. "I've tried to imagine myself going up and down this ministry, from room to room, knocking on the door of every chief of service, every director. I don't think I would have made it. Look at me. I'm already exhausted, just climbing up here to see you. I don't know what I would have done without people like you in Yaoundé."

"Don't worry about your file. You only have to be patient. The money you've given me will perform miracles, believe me. I'm quite confident the *bon de caisse* will be out in a week. I'll follow it myself. But to be on the safe side, I'll have to ask you to come back in two weeks. Today's already the 15th. Your *bon de caisse* may be out a few days before civil servants begin the long line-ups to collect their salaries in the banks."

"Two weeks? I've already run out of money, and I've spent a lifetime here in Yaoundé. My family will think something terrible has happened to me."

"Call them and tell them what's happening. Don't get too worried. In two weeks time, your suffering will be over. Imagine it! One moment you walk into the treasury, a retired man without a pension, the next moment, you come out with a millionaire's smile spread across your face." Mokube could not help laughing.

The old man too forced a smile. "Well, I guess there's nothing else for me to do than wait." He stood up and they shook hands. "I'll leave everything in your hands. It's not yet time to say thank you."

When he came out of Room 506, he took his time to descend the stairs. As he came down slowly, he began making some mental calculations. He wondered how much money he'll give everybody who had helped him in Yaoundé.

Mokube deserved about twenty five thousand francs. Will that be too small? Will the young man consider it an insult? And what about Kimbu? Did he deserve anything? And *Général*? A strange man. How does one say thank you to a strange man? Why does he not want me to come there again? Does he feel degraded in his container, in that bush there at Anguissa? Telling people their future and fortunes? Fooling around with a dead chameleon and the skull of a dead man? Thinks he can trick me? To send me away like that, with all that he's done for me? It must be the money. I remember mentioning eight million francs. That's what it is. Too much money for a fortune teller to comprehend. Poor fellow, the whole thing disturbs him. I saw prices of mechanized wheel-chairs the other day through the glazed glass of a shop window. Two hundred and fifty thousands. Sales! I will bargain and get a reduction. Will give him the surprise of his life. The wheelchair he uses looks old and dilapidated. I'll surprise him. That will teach him a lesson. Help a total stranger and send him away like that?

The car horns, the roar of the municipal buses and the noisy hustle and bustle of life in the street interrupted his thoughts. He tried to concentrate on the advancing line of yellow taxicabs. The vandals could hit him and leave him dead in the street. What would happen to the eight million francs? What will they do with his corpse? Of course, his nephew would identify him and make arrangements to send his body to Yambe. He dipped his right hand into the raffia bag and touched his I.D. card. He had to be more careful. It was getting to rush hour. He looked left and right before he crossed the street. He began walking down, towards *Poste Centrale*. It will be easier to get a taxi there to Anguissa. *In two weeks time ...* He tried to control his thoughts, to concentrate on the sidewalk in front of him. *In two weeks time .....*

FOURTEEN

The pensioner walked through the front entrance of the Treasury. He observed the wooden stands of the street vendors who sold envelopes, pens, customised forms, postcards and cigarettes. As he ascended the small flight of steps that led to the entrance of the treasury, his eye caught a variety of rosaries, crucifixes, statuettes of saints, and an assortment of religious memorabilia laid out on a big mat just by the front entrance of the building. He looked to his right and saw a beggar appealing for alms. The toothless old man held up a green plastic bowl to passers-by and shouted each time someone walked by. It was a half-cry, half-song, delivered in a rehearsed monotone.

Mokube had been visibly excited when the pensioner came to see him that morning at the ministry. "Your *bon de caisse* is out, Pa!" he cried. "Where have you been all these days?"

"You asked me to come back in two weeks time—"

"In two weeks time? It came out four days ago. Good heavens, Pa! Don't you realise what it means? Eight million, eight hundred thousand francs! In this time of crisis. You're a millionaire, Pa!" Mokube exclaimed, shaking the old man's hand vigorously.

"I ... I ... What?" the pensioner's voice faltered. He was stunned. His hands began to tremble. He used his right hand to support himself against the wall before he looked around for a chair and sat down.

Mokube looked worried and concerned. "Pa, are you alright?"

"No ... no ... I mean yes. I'm okay. I think I'm fine. Can I ...

Can I have some water to drink?" Mokube left the office and came back shortly with a glass of water. The old man drank it and took in a deep breath.

"Would you like another glass?"

"No. This is enough. Thank you. About the money, the *bon de caisse*, what do I do now?"

Mokube glanced at his watch. It's almost 10 AM. You'll have to go down to the treasury. At this time of the month, it's less busy. When you get to the front entrance turn to your left to a smaller building attached to the main block of the treasury itself. There's a man there called Ava Ze. Tell him I sent you. He'll tell you what to do."

"Would they need any other papers from me?" The old man could not recognise his own voice.

When Mokube replied, his voice appeared to come from a distance. "All they need is your identity card, that's all."

"Can I go there now, to ... to take the money?"

"Yes, yes. Of course. The *bon de caisse* was sent there three days ago. The money should be ready."

The pensioner stood up and readjusted the raffia bag across his left shoulder. "I'm going down to the treasury right away. I'll come back and see you as soon as I get the money. You've been very kind and helpful. I'll come and see you before your lunch break or in the afternoon."

Mokube walked to the door and opened it for the old man. As he walked out of the office, he murmured a few words of greetings to Mokube's co-workers.

The pensioner adjusted the raffia bag around his shoulder as he ascended the small mound that led up the smaller building attached to the treasury. It didn't take him long to find Ava Ze. Someone pointed him out from a distance. The old man walked up to his desk. It was littered with an assortment of files, papers and folders. He coughed slightly to attract Ava Ze's attention.

When Ava Ze looked up, the pensioner said, "You must be *Monsieur* Ava Ze. *Monsieur* Mokube at Finance sent me to you."

"*Ah, oui, Monsieur* Mokube. Yes. What can I do for you?"

I have a *bon de caisse* here in the treasury."

"What service, from which employer?"

"I'm retired."

"Ah, I see," Ava Ze said. "Were you with Territorial Administration or the army?"

"With the Public Service."

Ava Ze opened the bottom drawer and brought out a thick green file. "When was the *bon de caisse* sent here?"

"About three days ago," the pensioner said.

"About three days ago. Pension dossier. About three days ago." He kept on mumbling to himself as he rummaged through the files. "Is it an ordinary monthly pension payment or what?"

"My arrears for seven years."

"Did I hear you say arrears?"

"Yes."

"You should have told me that in the first place. About three days ago, three days ago." His fingers stopped moving for a moment. "Did you say three days ago?"

"Yes."

"And what's your name?"

"Wango. Lucas Wango."

"*Monsieur* Wango, *oui*?"

"Yes."

Ava Ze brought out a yellow form and looked at it. Then he whistled softly to himself. This time, he took a closer look at the old man. "Can I see your identity card, *Monsieur*?" The pensioner took out his identity card from the raffia bag and gave it to him. Ava Ze looked at the name on the card, glanced again at the old man before he gave it back to him. He picked up a bic pen from the table and gave it to the pensioner. He showed him a dotted line at the bottom of the form and asked him to sign his name.

The pensioner took the pen and looked closely at the form. It was a *bon de caisse*. It contained several rows of figures and complex calculations he could not comprehend. His eye fell on the last figure, the one at the end of the calculations. He saw the figure 8,850.000 towards the bottom of the page. Then he signed his signature and straightened up. Ava Ze tore off the yellow form and gave it to him. A pink duplicate was left in the file.

"Take this to the counter in the bigger building," Ava Ze said. "The main entrance is at the front. They'll have to see your national identity card."

The pensioner took the form and folded it into two. He thanked Ava Ze and walked out into the corridor. He noticed that Ava Ze was following him.

"Excuse me, *Monsieur*. Please forgive me. I need a little help," Ava Ze said. His voice was pleading, subdued.

"Help?"

"I have a little problem at home. I need some money to buy medication for my children."

"How much do you need?"

"Any amount, *Monsieur*, anything you give me."

"Okay. I'll come back and see you."

"*Merci, Monsieur. Merci beaucoup.* Please forgive me for disturbing you."

The pensioner smiled as he watched Ava Ze go back to his office. He skirted a small mound of earth and walked back the way he had come. He soon found himself at the front entrance of the treasury. He climbed another short flight of steps and came to a small lobby. Two policemen stopped him. One carried a gun; the other wielded a black truncheon.

"*Oui, Monsieur?*" the policeman with the truncheon said.

The pensioner reached inside his coat pocket and brought out the yellow form. The policeman looked at it, gave it back to the old man and pointed at a metal cage with a small window. "Go and see that man in the cage over there."

The upper compartment of the metal structure was made of a thin but tough wire mesh. Two other policemen leaned against the cage. As the pensioner got to the cage, the man inside thrust his hand through the small window. "Let me have the form."

The pensioner gave him the yellow form. The man looked at it and gave it back to the pensioner. "Give it to those officers there. They'll take your fingerprint," the man said, pointing at the two policemen.

"Over here, *Monsieur*," one of the policemen said.

The pensioner walked up to the policeman and stretched his left hand forward.

"The right hand, *Monsieur*. Not all the fingers, just the thumb. Be careful you don't stain yourself with the black ink." The policeman grabbed the old man's thumb and pressed it on a thick black metallic ink pad. Then he rolled the inked thumb gently on the bottom of the form, leaving a perfect thumb print on the paper. The policeman scribbled something over the print and handed the form to the man in the cage.

The man looked at the name on top of the form. "Can I see your national identity card, *Monsieur*?"

The pensioner took out his identity card and gave it to him. The man looked at the face on the photograph on the card and glanced at the old man. His eyes went back to the form as he looked at it more closely.

"All this is your money, *Monsieur*?"

"Yes. Is anything wrong?" There was a note of impatience in the pensioner's voice. He was becoming exasperated with the irritating questions about the amount of money on the *bon de caisse*. "It's my money, isn't it?" he yelled. "Why do you question me about my money?"

"I'm sorry, *Monsieur*. I didn't mean to annoy you. I was only asking. These are very hard times for all of us. I thought you could help me with two thousand francs for me to buy food and pay my taxi fare back home. Forgive me, *Monsieur*."

He took a piece of paper and scribbled the amount of money on the cash voucher. He signed the paper and handed it with the identity card to the old man. "Just walk through the big doors and go to any cashier whose counter is not occupied."

The old man put his identity card back into his breast pocket and walked confidently to the counter on his extreme left. A woman inside another cage behind the counter asked for the slip of paper and the pensioner's identity card.

The pensioner brought out his identity card, put the paper on it, and gave it to the woman.

She stared with wide eyes at the old man when she saw the amount of money on the paper. "*Mon Dieu!*" she exclaimed. "but you're a millionaire, *Monsieur!*"

"Yes," the old man said. "It's my money. It's for all the years I was retired without a pension."

She reached underneath the counter and brought out assorted bundles of ten thousand francs notes. First, she counted eight stacks of one million francs. Then she counted out eight wads of ten thousand francs that amounted to eight hundred thousand. Finally, she counted out fifty thousand in notes of five thousand francs. She verified the amount and looked at the old man.

"There you are, *Monsieur.*"

She pushed the money through the narrow opening on the counter. The old man grabbed the thick wads and threw them, one after the other, in the raffia bag. The woman gave him back his identity card. The pensioner took the fifty thousand francs and his identification card and stuffed them into the breast pocket of his coat. He looked at the woman briefly, turned round and walked out.

When he came to the lobby, the man in the cage and the

policemen were still there. He walked up to the man and gave him five thousand francs. He did not wait to hear the man's profuse thanks. He descended the stairs to the entrance of the building and went back to look for Ava Ze. He gave him five thousand francs and walked back to the front entrance of the treasury. He stood there for a while, contemplating whether he should take a taxi.

He clutched the raffia bag tightly against his body. The bag was full. He could feel it bulging against his tight grip. He looked at his watch. It was 11:45 AM. The traffic at the central roundabout was already building up. He knew it would be unsafe to take a taxi. They could attack him in the taxi. Someone had told him there were a lot of bogus taxis in the city that lured and then robbed unsuspecting victims. He made up his mind to walk all the way to Anguissa. He knew the toll his legs would have to pay, but he would endure it. It was much safer walking. If he was attacked he would shout for help. At least, people would see and hear him. In a taxi, he would be helpless.

As he came out into the street, he heard the blind beggar from the North who always sat in front of the treasury crying out for donations in his monotonous voice. He felt sorry for the man. But this was not the time for charity. He would try as much as possible not to attract attention to himself. He kept a watchful eye on the endless line of cars as he crossed over to the post office. He had one more crossing to do. He stood opposite the unfinished, abandoned multi-storeyed complex on the road to Mvog-Ada, watching the traffic, waiting for a chance to cross the busy road.

As the long rows of cars slowed down to a crawl, he crossed over quickly. He turned right and began climbing the hill to Mvog-Ada. Now and then, he looked behind to see whether anyone was following him. He settled down to a steady pace after he ascended the hill. He looked behind and around him. No one was following him. The road was busy as usual. No one was paying any attention to him.

As he approached College Privé Montesquieu, opposite the M.R.S. petrol station, he saw a group of five boys beating up a child. They were big boys, about 14 or 15 years old. The child was barely six. Three of the bigger boys had the child pinned on the pavement, face down. Another boy sat on his back, and the other two boys were kicking and slapping him at the same time. The child was crying out for help. Nobody paid attention to him or to what was going on. The pensioner approached the group.

"Hey, leave the child alone." He came forward and began shoving the youngsters away with his right hand. He pulled one of them and smacked him on the head. "What are you doing? Leave the child alone."

He did not notice the rider of a Yamaha motorbike who had kept a discreet distance behind him on the road. The old man was now struggling with the boys, trying to dislodge them from the child who was still sobbing on the pavement. The bike rider changed gears and accelerated. In one swift motion, he seized the raffia bag from the pensioner's hand, tearing the bag off and leaving its frail straps on the old man's shoulder. The force of the motion spun the old man round. He staggered forward and fell down on the pavement. He managed to regain his composure immediately. No one seemed to notice anything. People were still walking up and down the street as if nothing had happened.

"Hey!" the pensioner screamed, "my bag!" The words were stuck in his throat. He tried to run after the bike. He could see it ahead of him, in the distance. The rider wore a helmet with an opaque glass screen. He glanced back momentarily at the old man, took a bend, and disappeared.

Slowly, the pensioner lowered his left hand. It was still knotted in a grip. Only the bag's torn fibre straps remained in his hand. He remembered the child and turned round to see what was happening to him. There was no one on the pavement. The children had all vanished.

It took a while before the impact of what had happened sunk into his mind. He felt dizzy. He began sweating profusely. The sweat poured down his armpits, neck, and face. He felt like urinating. For a brief moment, everything came to a stop. He looked around him again. He did not know where he was. He was dazed, confused, and stunned. Something inside him snapped. A bemused, distrait smile gradually spread across the furrowed features of his face. With the smile came an uneasy peace, a disquieting serenity his mind tried to comprehend. He burst into a laugh. It was a carefree, senseless outburst of purposeless mirth. He turned round again and began walking in the opposite direction, from where he had come. That was when he felt the wetness between his thighs. He was not even aware that his trousers were soaked in his own urine. Somewhere inside him, he remembered his pension file. Where was he? What was happening to his thoughts? He shook his head and wiped his face with his right hand. He looked around him again and fixed his gaze towards the downtown area. Where was he? Of course, he was in Mvog-Ada. How silly of him. His file was still in the Ministry of Finance. He should be in the ministry, not here in the streets of Mvog-Ada.

He had no problem crossing the street. He began walking in the opposite direction, towards the downtown area, from where he had come. He was surprised at the clarity of his own thoughts, the heightened sharpness of his consciousness. He was now between Camtel and Casino. He kept a steady walking pace along the 20th May Avenue, making his way towards the Hilton. He passed in front of the Prime Minister's office and began walking upwards, towards the Ministry of Finance.

He went straight to the front entrance when he finally got to the Ministry. It was almost 4 PM and workers in the Ministry had started leaving the building. He went through the lobby of the Ministry and began climbing the staircase to the first floor.

As he passed the landing of the first floor, he met a man cleaning the stairs.

"Hey, where do you think you're going? Don't you see I'm cleaning the floor?" the man yelled.

The pensioner ignored him.

"Am I not talking to you?"

"I'm going to see the director. My file is up there with him."

"Which director?" the cleaner demanded. "Everybody is going home. The Ministry is already closed. There's no one up there. You'll have to come back tomorrow."

The old man looked at his watch. It was almost 4 PM. "He's waiting for me," he said. "He asked me to come in the evening."

The cleaner shrugged and resumed cleaning the stairs.

It was a tedious climb, but he went up slowly, inevitably. He passed the second floor, third floor, fourth floor. When he got to the landing on the fifth floor, he rested for a while to regain his strength and breath. Then he began walking up and down the corridor, trying the handles of each door, searching for the director who was keeping his pension file.

He knew the workers were in their offices. So they had locked the doors from inside because they didn't want to see him? The bastards! He'll show them. He began shouting obscenities at the top of his voice and banging loudly on the doors along the entire corridor. He went back to the landing and noticed a big open window for the first time. He pushed his head through the open space and looked down. There were still a lot of cars in the parking lot. He felt a chilly breeze caress his face. It was refreshing. So refreshing. At the same time, he heard several voices and footsteps running up the stairs. Someone was shouting: "Who's up there? What are you doing there?" The voices became more audible, the approaching footsteps more threatening.

He looked down again through the window. It was at that moment that he saw *Général*. He was in his wheelchair. "I'm up here!" the pensioner shouted. Will he hear him? "Up here on the fourth floor!" he shouted again. *Général* looked up and saw him. Yes, he had seen him. He beckoned him to come down and meet him. Even from this distance, he saw *Général*'s lips move. He heard him say, *Yes, to the container. Come down and let's go to the container.* It was an invitation he could not decline. *I didn't mean to send you away like that,* he heard *Général* say. *I have connections everywhere. Even if the file is lost, I'll get someone to resurrect it. I'll give you more fiscal stamps…*

The footsteps pounded up the stairs. The pensioner lifted his right foot and heaved the rest of his body after him. He raised himself slowly and stood on the window ledge. The wind was fanning his face. It felt so invitingly cool, so exhilarating. Two guards and the cleaner appeared on the landing. He looked down again and saw the inviting face of *Général*.

"What the hell is he doing up there?" a voice said. "Stop him!"

No one could come between him and *Général* now. He just had a brief moment to see *Général*'s face expand into a half-smile before he leaped into the open air. It was *Général*'s inviting smile that filled his consciousness as he hurtled down. Nobody could stop him now, not even the director. The sudden rush of air against his face and body filled his mind with a long-sought freedom. No one could stop him now; nothing could prevent him from meeting *Général*.

FIFTEEN

The siren of an ambulance coming from the direction of the Central Hospital. The ear-piercing siren of a police squad car dispatched from the Seventh District police station. The ever-increasing crowd of inquisitive onlookers. Two photographers from *Mutations* and *Le Messager* newspapers are taking photographs. Another reporter from *Cameroon Tribune* is observing the scene. Squads of producers and cameramen from CRTV, Canal 2, and STV are already filming the accident scene and the crowd. A Canal 2 female reporter is talking to a young hawker of about twenty-five who claims he saw the dead man fall from the building.

"What exactly did you see?" the reporter wanted to know.

"I saw the man flying in the air. It happened so fast, so quickly."

"Where were you?"

"Not too far from here."

"How faraway from the location of the tragedy?"

"I can't tell, but I wasn't far from where the man landed on the ground."

"What were you doing at the time of the accident?"

"What was I doing? I was selling sliced pineapples. That's what I do for a living. That's my push truck over there."

"Did you see anybody up there on the window ledge from which he fell?"

"Can't tell. Soon after he flew through the air, just before he hit the ground, I thought I saw two people looking down from that window up there."

"So you saw him jump from the window."

"Yes."

"Do you think it was an accident or a crime?"

"Well, who would want to kill an old man like that?" the hawker wondered. "It's probably an accident."

The reporter saw two policemen come out of the squad car with its flashing red and amber lights. "Thank you very much," she said to the hawker." She turned round and shoved the microphone in front of the advancing police officers who were pushing their way through the crowd. The first policeman brushed aside the microphone and moved to where the mutilated body of the dead man lay.

"Go back to the car and bring the tape. We have to cordon off the accident scene," Superintendent Frederic Onana said.

"I'll do that at once," Inspector Manuel Nana replied.

"When you return, push back the crowd. There're too many people here. If we don't send them back they'll obstruct our investigation."

Three minutes later Inspector Nana came back. He unrolled the red and white tape and cordoned off the area where the dead man lay. "Okay!" he shouted at the top of his voice. "Move back five metres from the police tape! Come on, move! Keep moving! That's good. Keep moving! Where's the man the Canal 2 reporter was talking to?" The hawker raised his hand. "Alright, come over here. We'll like to talk to you." There was a murmur in the crowd. The hawker stepped forward and joined the two policemen.

Inspector Nana brought out a pen and small notebook from his breast pocket. Superintendent Onana came close to the young man and began questioning him. Just then a black Mercedes E280 pulled up on the pavement. A man in a chauffeur's uniform and cap came out of the car, opened the boot, and brought out a wheelchair. The chauffeur opened the right side of the Mercedes and placed the chair close to the door. He helped *Général* out and placed him in the wheelchair.

"Take me to the two policemen over there, behind the police tape," *Général* ordered.

"Right away, *Général*."

Superintendent Onana and Inspector Nana saw *Général* coming towards them. "Stop right there!" Inspector Nana said. "There's been an accident. You're not allowed to come beyond the police tape."

Superintendent Onana stopped talking to the hawker. "Go back to the crowd. If we need you, we'll talk to you again." The young man went back and joined the bystanders.

Superintendent Onana turned to *Général* and said with authority, "What brings you here? Do you know you're obstructing a police investigation?"

"I know the dead man," *Général* said.

"You know him!" Inspector Nana exclaimed. "How? Where?"

"He was my friend. I was helping him recover his pension file."

As they spoke, the ambulance from the Central Hospital came close to the sidewalk and stopped. Two paramedics came out of the ambulance. One of them held a white body bag. The two men ran towards the policemen.

"No hurry," Superintendent Onana told the paramedics. "There's been an accident. The man is dead. Probably in his late sixties. Take the body to the military hospital mortuary." The two paramedics carried the bag to the accident scene, unzipped it, lifted the pensioner's body and began putting what was left of the dead man into the white bag.

"Let me have his I.D card and any other documents he has on him," Superintendent Onana told the paramedics.

One of the paramedics walked up to the Superintendent and handed him a national I.D. card. "This is all we found on him."

Superintendent Onana took the I.D. card. "All right," he said to *Général*. "You'll come with us to the police station. We want to get a detailed picture of the dead man—who he was, where he came from, how you knew him. It will help us determine what made him jump down to his death."

"Or who pushed him off the building," Inspector Nana added. "He may have equally been pushed from the building."

"No problem," *Général* said. "My chauffeur will follow your squad car. Take me back to the car and follow the officers to the Seventh District police station," *Général* told his chauffeur.

"As you say, *Général.*"

At the police station, the Superintendent invited *Général* to his office instead of taking him to the interrogation room. The chauffeur rolled the wheelchair into the Superintendent's office and left *Général* inside. Inspector Nana was already in the office, sitting down on one of the chairs.

"The Superintendent will send a policeman to call you when I'm finished," *Général* told the chauffeur.

Superintendent Onana closed the door, went to his desk and sat down. "I don't want to waste your time," he told *Général*. "I just want the bare facts to enable me to close this investigation. Nothing but facts. This is not the first case of suicide we've had in the Ministry of Finance. We've had five cases this year alone. How did you know the dead man?"

"I first met him in Anguissa. In front of the *Rio bar d'Anguissa.* He followed me to my headquarters in the evening for a consultation." Inspector Nana jotted *Général's* statement in a bloc notebook.

"When was this?" the Superintendent inquired.

"I'm not quite sure," *Général* said. "About three weeks ago."

"You said earlier that you were helping him recover his pension dossier," Superintendent Onana went on.

"Yes. His pension file was missing in the Public Service for seven years. That's why he came to Yaoundé. I simply provided him with contacts in the Ministry and the *prefecture* to help him reconstitute his lost file."

"Where were you when the incident took place?"

"In my headquarters, at Anguissa."

"Do you have any witnesses to confirm this?"

"Of course," *Général* laughed. "My men are still there, waiting for me in the container. You can go right now and talk to them."

"That will not be necessary," Superintendent Onana said. "And how did you know about the accident? You came to the Ministry quite quickly, almost at the same time that we did."

"Someone called me on my cell phone minutes after the accident occurred."

"Can we know who?"

"One of my multiple contacts. He remains anonymous."

"I see," Superintendent Onana said. "Well, this is off the record," he said, turning to Inspector Nana. Inspector Nana closed the notebook in which he had been taking down notes. "Where will he be buried? Has he got relatives here in Yaoundé? Someone who can take the corpse to wherever he came from?"

"He did mention a maternal nephew, something like that. I don't know where he lives. I'll foot the mortuary bills no matter how long he stays in there."

"Oh," Superintendent Onana said, forcing a grin on his face, "so you've become a philanthropist too, have you?"

"You could say that," *Général* said.

"Where did he come from, the dead man?"

"From Yambe, in the North West Region. I intend to make a radio announcement tomorrow so that his relatives, either here in Yaoundé or his hometown, will hear the sad news. I'll also leave my cell phone number in the announcement in case someone in his family decides to contact me."

"How soon do you think you can get a response?" Inspector Nana wanted to know.

"Difficult to say. But once the announcement is made, I'm sure someone will call me within twenty-four or forty-eight hours."

The Superintendent glanced at his watch. "Almost 6 PM already? How time flies. I guess we're done. If there's additional information we require in our investigations, I'll let you know. Thank you for your cooperation."

"It's me to thank you," *Général* said. "Can you tell my chauffeur to come and take me out of here?" he asked Inspector Nana.

Inspector Nana went out and came back with the chauffeur. The chauffeur wheeled *Général* to the car, placed him in the backseat before he folded the wheelchair and put it in the boot. He went round, entered the car and started the engine.

"Where to now, *Général*?"

"To Anguissa. Biyem-Assi and the rest of the men are waiting for me to give their report of the day."

The chauffeur pulled the car slowly out of the police parking lot and entered the slow line of cars that would take him past *Post Centrale* to Anguissa.

By the time *Général* reached the container, it was already 7 PM. After the report of the day, the rest of the men left. He asked Etoudi, Mokolo, and the accountant to stay behind.

"I need to buy a coffin," he said, "a good coffin. Etoudi, have you any idea where we can buy one?"

"Yes, *Général*. There're several good places in town."

He turned to the accountant. "How much would a good coffin cost?"

"Depends on the wood, *Général*. A bubinga coffin is the most expensive. They can get up to eight hundred thousand francs. It's the best wood. A bibolo, sapele, iroko, or mahogany coffin will cost much less. But they're equally good."

"I also want you to find out how much it will cost to hire a hearse to the North West."

"Where to in the North West, Général?"

"To Yambe. It's a small town about 35 kilometres north east

of Bamenda."

"How soon do you want this information, *Général*," the accountant asked.

"As soon as possible, in the next three or four days. You should go and find out about hiring a hearse to Yambe. Etoudi and Mokolo, the two of you should find out about the coffin. Negotiate the prices with the undertakers. An iroko or mahogany coffin will do. Select a good one."

Two days later, *Général* got the first phone call following his radio announcement. The caller said his name was Kemcha. "I heard a radio announcement concerning my uncle who lived with us here in Anguissa. We've not seen him for two days now."

"There was an accident—" *Général* began.

"An accident? Where? What happened? Where is he?"

"I'm sorry," *Général* said. "I'm so sorry. He died. He's in the mortuary."

The man screamed and the line went silent. When the man called again two hours later, his voice was hoarse. *Général* heard a woman sobbing in the background.

"Where did you say Pa was?"

"In the mortuary, at the military hospital. His removal will be at 9 AM on Friday, that's after tomorrow."

"Who has made the arrangements? Where will he be buried?"

"I have. I'm his friend. His body will be taken to Yambe, his hometown. Don't forget to come to the mortuary at 8 AM on Friday morning."

Kemcha, his wife Eli, and their eldest son met *Général* at the military hospital mortuary on Friday. They came to the mortuary before 8 AM. They were surprised to see the expensive mahogany coffin in which the old man's remains were put. They were even more astonished when the coffin was carried by four men—Bosco, Etoudi, Gaston, and Mokolo—and put into a Mercedes Benz hearse outside the mortuary. Two other men carried wreaths which they put in the hearse.

Général said, "I've arranged with two of my men, Etoudi and Bosco, to go with the corpse to Yambe. Let me know whether you want to go with them."

"To go with them?" Kemcha asked. "I don't have money. I would have liked to go with the corpse to Yambe."

Général dipped his right hand into his shirt pocket and brought out a thick wad of notes. He counted fifty thousand francs and gave the money to Kemcha. "Here, take this. It should cover your expenses to Yambe and back."

Kemcha counted the money and was taken aback by the amount. "All of this? For me alone?"

"Yes," *Général* said.

Kemcha looked at *Général* with admiration and respect. "Thank you, sir. Thank you very much."

"Okay," Bosco said, "time to go." Bosco and Etoudi sat with the driver in the front of the hearse while Kemcha sat on another seat behind the driver. The driver started the engine and put on the siren. The hearse came out into the road and gathered speed through the early morning traffic on its way to Bamenda.

Later that day, a dense fog descended over the city. Yaoundé had never experienced such a fog before. The city had experienced an occasional fog, usually in the early hours of the morning; but it typically dissipated as soon as the sun came out. This afternoon's fog enveloped the entire city like a thick white blanket. TV and radio stations devoted the first part of their news to the fog, talking about how it had shrouded the entire city, advising drivers to put on their headlights, and to drive slowly and carefully. The fog was so dense in Anguissa that *Général* could not see the trees and small bushes that surrounded the container.

For the first time in several years, *Général* switched off his cell phone and spent the day alone in the container thinking about his life in Yaoundé. He was unsettled as his mind wandered from one thought to the other, in no particular sequence. He thought about the first time he saw the old man in front of the *Rio bar d'Anguissa*, then his thoughts switched to Assuma, the deceased director who owed him six months rents. He thought of the time he spent with Marie-Noel, the university girl, who provided him so much erotic pleasure and stimulation. His thoughts moved to the city again. How the city had betrayed him, and how he took advantage of the multifaceted opportunities that Yaoundé offered to talented people who were willing to survive against all odds. Then his mind settled on the old man's mutilated body, where he had landed on the ground at the Ministry of Finance.

He looked out the window of the container. The fog was still there. It had a woolly, eerie texture to it. When Mokolo and the rest of his men came to the container that evening, they found him in a gloomy mood. For the first time, he cancelled the report of the day and asked the men to go back to their homes and leave him alone, except Mvog-Mbi and his chauffeur.

At about 9 PM, he called Mvog-Mbi and the chauffeur to take him to the car which was parked opposite the *Rio bar d'Anguissa*. When they brought him to the road, they put him in the car. Mvog-Mbi reminded him of his appointment with Marie-Noel.

He did not answer. He did not even hear what Mvog-Mbi said. He was lost in his own thoughts. He thought about what he had achieved in Yaoundé all these years. The car moved on steadily to Total Melen, going past the University Teaching Hospital. Something was stirring inside him. He could not figure out what it was. Martina had mentioned something about his being afraid to look at his face in the mirror, about his being scared to confront himself. Was that it? Was that what it was? A beam of light suddenly appeared in the thick miasma of darkness that had shrouded him.

Mvog-Mbi's excited voice snapped him out of his thoughts. 'Look, *Général!* The fog is clearing! It's fading away. I can't believe it!"

"Stop the car!" *Général* shouted. "Stop right now!" The chauffeur slammed on the brakes and the car came to a hasty stop. "Where are we? What part of the town is this?"

"We're in Obili, *Général*."

"In Obili? What are we doing in Obili? How did we get here?"

"Marie-Noel—" Mvog-Mbi tried to remind him. "That's where you're going."

"Marie-Noel? Turn the car round and drive to Bastos."

"To Bastos, *Général*?" The chauffeur was confused.

"I said to Bastos. Take me to Martina's place. Take me there now!" He was ready to reclaim his manhood tonight. He was going to prove Martina wrong. He would surprise her. He would show her tonight that he was no longer afraid to be a man. He had confronted himself in the thick fog and wrestled with those malevolent demons that prevented him from accepting himself for who he was, what he was supposed to be. Kevin will see and know his father for the first time this night. Even if the boy was asleep, he would wake him up. From now on, he will abandon his three bedroom house in Cité Verte, give it out for rent or sell it and move in with Martina in Bastos. He'll buy Martina's house. They will own it. It would be their house.

The chauffeur made a U-turn and began the long drive to Bastos.

The End

GLOSSARY OF FRENCH AND PIDGIN ENGLISH PHRASES

FRENCH PHRASES

Monsieur
Sir
Oui
Yes
Mais oui
Of course
Oui, Monsieur
Yes, sir
Mais, Monsieur
But, sir
Monsieur Akuma
Mr Akuma
Ah, oui, Monsieur Mokube
Oh yes, Mr Mokube
Madame
Madam
Monsieur
Sir/Mr
Cent cent, deux places
A hundred francs for both of us

Beignet
oil-fried puff balls
Bouillon de deux cents
pap for two hundred francs
Mon Dieu
Good heavens
Composition du dossier
Compilation of file
Demande timbrée à 1000 FCFA
Stamped application of 1000 FCFA
Copie act de mariage
Copy of marriage certificate
Copie acte de naissance des enfants mineurs
Copy of birth certificate for dependent children
Certificat de vie collectif des enfants mineurs
Collective life certificate for dependent children
Certificat de scolarité des enfants mineurs
School attendance certificate for dependent children
Certificat de domicile
Certificate of residence
Bulletin de Solde
Pay slip
Voilà
That's it
Oui, Monsieur. Qu'est-ce qu'il y a encore?
Yes, sir. What do you want again?
Ah, mon Dieu! Mais vous les Anglophones, vous derangez trop
Good gracious! You English-speaking people are quite troublesome.
S'il vous plaît, Monsieur
Please, sir
Bureau
Department

Chef de service-adjoint
Deputy head of department
Sous directeur
Sub-director
Directeur-adjoint
Deputy director
Courrier
Mail room
Courrier centrale
Central mail service
Courrier solde
Mail service in the department of salaries
Arêté
Ordinance
Contrôle financier
Financial control
La radio
The broadcasting house
C'est grave, Monsieur Wango. C'est très grave
It's serious, Mr Wango, very serious
La nourriture est bonne ici, eh
The food is so good here, eh.
Vraiment, mais vous les Anglophones, vous vivez bien ici à Kumba
My word! You English-speaking people live so well here in Kumba.
Prefecture
Administrative district
Préfet
Senior District Officer
Sous-Préfet
Assistant District Officer
Bonsoir, mon beau
Good evening, my handsome one

Patron
Boss
Mon Commissaire
Superintendent
Merci, Monsieur. Merci Beaucoup
Thank you, sir. Thank you very much.
Bonjour, Madame
Good morning, madam
Bonjour, Monsieur
Good morning, sir
hommes à tout faire
odd job men
Primes
bonuses
le chasseur
the hunter
bon de caisse
pay voucher
bon d'engagement
Commitment voucher
Tu connais où on peut trouver le chasseur?
Where can we find the hunter?
Mais oui. Il doit se cacher quelque part
Of course. He should be around somewhere.
Direction du budget *Budget management*
Service de Titre Règlements
Payment document service
Direction de la Solde: Service de Pension
Department of salaries: Pension Service
Renseignement
Information office
Service du Retrait des bons de caisse
Pay voucher withdrawal service

Courrier ordinateur
Computer mail service
Poste Centrale
Central post office

PIDGIN ENGLISH PHRASES

Bamenda, one man
Bamenda, one more person
Motor done full oh!
The bus is full!
Time for go!
Time to go!
No waste my time!
Don't waste my time!
Moof money for pocket, pay your bus fare
Take the money from your pocket, pay your bus fare
Driver wait. I beg driver wait oh. I beg wait for me
Please driver, wait for me
Yes, sah, where you de go?
Yes, sir, where are you going?
I de go for Bamenda
I'm going to Bamenda
Next bus. You go enter na next bus
You'll take the next bus
I get urgent business for Bamenda
I've got urgent business in Bamenda
No sah, I no fit
I'm sorry sir, I can't take you
Dat one na overload
We'll be charged with overloading the bus
Gendarme and police dem go take all we money for road
Gendarmes and the police will take all our money at road blocks

I beg, conductor
Please, conductor
I go add one extra thousand for the regular fare
I'll add an additional thousand francs on the regular fare
Go talk for driver
Talk to the driver
Make e enter! Squeezam anywhere!
Let him in. Squeeze him anywhere
Oya, driver, we go
Okay, driver, let's go
Bouillon de deux cents
Pap for two hundred francs
You be stranger for Yawinde
Is this your first time in Yaoundé?
You commot which place for Bamenda?
What part of Bamenda do you come from?
I be Barforchu woman
I'm from Barforchu
My man commot for Babanki
My husband is from Babanki
You do stay for whosai?
Where do you live?
Come chop beignet and drink pap here every morning
Come and eat beignet and drink pap here every morning
All man pikin dem de chop na for here
Most men come and eat here
Hey, my broda, money fine oh!
Hey, my brother, money is good!

ABOUT THE AUTHOR

B a'bila Mutia is a Cameroonian author, poet, and playwright. He holds an MA in Creative Writing from the University of Windsor, Canada. His short stories and poetry have been featured in anthologies and reviews worldwide. He is the author of *Whose Land?* (Longman children's fiction); "*Rain*" (short story) in *A Window on Africa*; "*The Miracle*" (short story) in *The Heinemann Book of Contemporary African Short Stories*; "*The Spirit Machine*" (short story) in *The Spirit Machine and Other New Short Stories from Cameroon* and *Coils of Mortal Flesh* (poetry). In 1993, Mutia was a guest of the Berlin Academy of Arts for an international short story reading. In September 2011, Mutia's play, *The Road to Goma*, was among six winners of the African Playwriting Project sponsored by the London National Theatre Studio where excerpts of his play were staged by professional actors. He has lived in Lagos and Benin City (Nigeria), Windsor and Halifax (Canada). He currently resides in Yaoundé, Cameroon where he is a lecturer in African literature and creative writing at the *Ecole Normale Supérieure*.

Printed in the United States
By Bookmasters